An Island

An Island

A Novel

Karen Jennings

HOGARTH

LONDON   NEW YORK

Published in the United States by Hogarth, an imprint of Random House, a division of Penguin Random House LLC, New York.

HOGARTH is a trademark of the Random House Group Limited, and the H colophon is a trademark of Penguin Random House LLC.

Originally published in Great Britain by Holland House Books in 2020. This edition published by arrangement with Holland House Books in conjunction with their duly appointed agent Agence Deborah Druba, Paris, France. All rights reserved.

Library of Congress Cataloging-in-Publication Data
Names: Jennings, Karen, 1982– author.
Title: An island: a novel / Karen Jennings.
Description: First edition. | New York, New York: Hogarth, [2022] |
Originally published in Great Britain by Holland House Books in 2020.
Identifiers: LCCN 2021049281 (print) | LCCN 2021049282 (ebook) |
ISBN 9780593446522 (hardcover; acid-free paper) |
ISBN 9780593446539 (ebook)
Subjects: LCGFT: Novels.
Classification: LCC PR9369.4.J48 I85 2022 (print) |
LCC PR9369.4.J48 (ebook) | DDC 823/.92—dc23/eng/20211008
LC record available at https://lccn.loc.gov/2021049281
LC ebook record available at https://lccn.loc.gov/2021049282

PRINTED IN THE UNITED STATES OF AMERICA ON ACID-FREE PAPER

randomhousebooks.com

1 3 5 7 9 8 6 4 2

First US Edition

Art by mikeosphoto/stock.adobe.com

The First Day

It was the first time that an oil drum had washed up on the scattered pebbles of the island shore. Other items had arrived over the years—ragged shirts, bits of rope, cracked lids from plastic lunch boxes, braids of synthetic material made to resemble hair. There had been bodies, too, as there was today. The length of it stretched out beside the drum, one hand reaching forward as though to indicate that they had made the journey together and did not now wish to be parted.

Samuel saw the drum first, through one of the small windows as he made his way down the inside of the lighthouse tower that morning. He had to walk with care. The stone steps were ancient, worn smooth, their valleyed centers ready to trip him up. He had inserted metal handholds into those places where the cement had allowed, but the rest of the descent was done with arms outstretched, fingers brushing the rough sides in support.

The drum was plastic, the blue of workers' overalls, and remained in sight, bobbing in the flow, during his hastening to the shore. The body he saw only once he arrived. He sidestepped it, walking a tight circle around the drum. It was fat as a president, without any visible cracks or punctures.

He lifted it carefully. It was empty; the seal had held. Yet despite being light, the thing was unwieldy. It would not be possible with his gnarled hands to grip that smooth surface and carry it across the jagged pebbles, over the boulders, and then up along the sandy track, through scrub and grasses, to the headland where the cottage sat alongside the tower. Perhaps if he fetched a rope and tied the drum to his back, he could avoid using the ancient wooden barrow with its wheel that splintered and caught on the craggy beach, often overturning as a result of its own weight.

Yes, carrying the drum on his back would be the best option. Afterward, in the yard, he would hunt out the old hacksaw that lived among sacking and rotting planks. He would rub the rust from the blade, sharpen it as best he could, and saw the top off the drum, then place it in an outside corner of the cottage where the guttering overflowed, so that it could catch rainwater for use in his vegetable garden.

Samuel let the drum fall. It lurched on the uneven surface, thudding against the arm of the corpse. He had forgotten about that. He sighed. All day it would take him to dispose of the body. All day. First moving it, then the burial, which was impossible anyway on the rocky island with its thin layer of sand. The only option was to cover it with stones, as he had done with others in the past. Yet it was such a large body. Not in breadth, but in its length. Twice as long as the drum, as though the swell and ebb of the sea had mangled it into this unnatural, elongated form.

The arms were strong, disproportionate to the naked torso's knuckled spine and sharp ribs. Small, fine black curls formed patches on each shoulder blade, and more colored the base of the back where it met his gray denim shorts. The same curls, small, too small for a man of his size, grew on his legs and toes, across his forearms and between the joints of his fingers. They unsettled Samuel. They were the hairs of a newborn animal or of a baby who had stayed too long in the womb. What had the sea birthed here on these stones?

Already, as the midmorning sun was rising, the curls were silvering with salt crystals. His hair, too, was gray where sand had settled in it. Grains adhered to the only portion of the man's face that was visible—part of his forehead, a closed eye. The rest of the face was pressed into his shoulder.

Samuel tutted. That would have to wait. First he would tend to the drum, then next morning, if the body hadn't drifted back into the sea, he would have to break some of the island's rocks, creating enough pieces to cover it.

There had been thirty-two of these washed-up

corpses during the twenty-three years that he had been lighthouse keeper. All thirty-two nameless, unclaimed. In the beginning, when the government was new, crisp with promises, when all was still chaos, and the dead and missing of a quarter of a century under dictatorial rule were being sought, Samuel had reported the bodies. The first time officials had come out, with clipboards and a dozen body bags, combing the island for shallow graves, for remains lodged between boulders, for bones and teeth that had become part of the gravelly sand.

"You understand," the woman in charge had said, as she looked down at a scuff mark on her patent-leather heels, "we have made promises. We must find all those who suffered under the Dictator so that we can move forward, nationally. In a field outside the capital, my colleagues found a grave of at least fifty bodies. Another colleague discovered the remains of seven people who had been hanged from trees in the forest. They were still hanging, you understand, all this time later. Who knows how many we will find here? I am certain it will be many. This is an ideal dumping ground."

"Do you think so?"

"Oh yes, just look around." She waved at the view. "No one for miles. No one to see or hear or do anything at all." She leaned closer, lowered her voice. "They say there's been some talk that he had secret camps, like concentration camps, where he sent dissenters to die. Of course, we don't know yet if it is absolutely true. We haven't found evidence of that, but this could well have been such a place, don't you think? Isn't this a place where you would send someone to die?"

Samuel did not reply, and the woman had already turned from him, was calling to a member of her team, tapping her watch. "Keep looking," she said after the man had shaken his head. She faced Samuel again and said, "Once we've found the bodies, that's the time when the healing will begin, for the nation, for us all. We can't heal until then. We need the bodies."

When the crew returned one by one, empty-handed, with only the washed-up corpse to show for a day's work, she rushed to the boat, her departure abrupt, without the courtesy of a goodbye. Samuel did not hear from her, nor from her department. He did not know what happened to the dead man, or who he might have been.

Months later, perhaps a year, he found three small bodies washed up side by side. A young boy, a girl, a baby in a blanket. In those days, the lighthouse's radio still worked and he'd contacted the shore to report. The woman called him back, her voice clipped by the static.

"What color are they?"

"What?"

"What color are they? The bodies. What color?"

He was silent.

"What I am asking is, are they darker than us—their skin—that is what I want to know. Are they darker than you or me?"

"I think so."

"And their faces? Are they longer? What are their cheekbones like?"

"I don't know. They're children. They look like children."

"Listen, we're busy people. We have real crimes to deal with. Actual atrocities, you understand. We cannot come out to the island every time another country's refugees flee and drown. It's not our problem."

"What must I do with them then?"

"Do what you like. We don't want them."

By then he had already started his vegetable garden beside the cottage, had used his wages to import soil from the mainland, had ordered seeds and clippings. And to protect all of that new growth, he had begun to fashion a dry-stone wall around it. He gathered all the brick-sized stones of the island, fitting them together one on top of the other, until they were high enough, stretched far enough to form a barrier. After that he ordered a sledgehammer and broke apart the many rocks and boulders that composed the coastline, using the rubble in his construction. Slowly the island began to change shape. Had a helicopter been in the habit of flying over, its pilot would note the widening of the small bays, the curves where serrated edges had once been.

Samuel continued with the wall along the perimeter of the island until everything was encircled. It was into this outer wall that he began to introduce the bodies. Most times before burying them, Samuel went through their pockets for objects of identification, but there had never been anything of significance. Not beyond an old man's fist, lumpen with a wad of foreign money squeezed to pulp in his grip. Samuel had buried him with it. He selected spots for the corpses in those sections of the wall that were farthest from the cottage, where the smell of their decay would not reach him. Still, they attracted gulls that for weeks hovered and cawed around the wall, trying to peck their way in. With time he learned to make these parts sturdier, so that they bulged a little around their contents. Even so, sometimes the gulls managed to break through and pick at the body inside. In those places where corpses were left to disintegrate unaided, the stones often collapsed.

Samuel half nudged, half kicked the body where it lay beside the drum. The impact caused the arm to shift, the head to roll from its position and reveal the face. Both eyes opened briefly. The throat growled and fingers on the extended hand twitched, tapping a pebble beneath them.

Samuel shuffled backward. "Hello," he said softly. Then, "Hello."

The man did not move again, but there was now the visible slow throbbing of a pulse in his neck. Up-down, up-down it beat as the sea hissed onto the pebbles and away again.

Samuel counted. Fifty beats. Two hundred. Three hundred and fifty. At five hundred he turned to the plastic drum, wrapped his arms around its middle and lifted it awkwardly in front of him, unable to see as he stumbled up the shore beyond the high-water mark. He laid the drum on its side, chocked it with pebbles, and then returned to the body, counting one hundred more pulses before making his way up toward the headland through the well-worn paths that never altered.

The gulls had arrived while he was gone. They stood a few meters from the man, calling uncertainly, darting forward with low heads. One of them flapped its wings, approached the right leg, and took an awkward peck at the man's shorts. But by then Samuel was on the sandy path, pushing the heavy wheelbarrow in front of him.

"Get away there! Go on! Get away!"

The birds rose, hovering low as Samuel struggled through the boulders to the pebbled shore. He stopped beside the body and removed some rope from the bowl of the wheelbarrow, walking to where he had left the drum. He tied the rope around it, twice across the middle, twice along its height, and fastened it to a tall boulder. There were no trees on this part of the island, only dry, leafless scrub that snapped if touched.

He returned to the man, put a hand under each armpit, and tried to pull him toward the wheelbarrow. The body would not move. Samuel grunted as he continued to tug, hoping that with persistence the body could be yanked loose from whatever held it in place. Soon his arms were aching, the small of his back aflame. He cried out, falling backward as a pebble came loose underfoot. Now the body was on top of him. A foreigner's damp hair, a foreigner's sweat and breath. He pushed the weight off, lifted himself up. The hair under the man's arms was coarse and long. As Samuel heaved, he felt himself pulling out those rough long strands: they stuck to the sweat on his wrists and forearms, working their way under his fingernails. He rinsed his hands and arms in the sea, before grabbing hold of the man again.

After several minutes, he was able to lift the shoulders onto the wheelbarrow. His buttocks leaned against the wood as he caught his breath. Then he moved around to the side of the wheelbarrow, dragging the torso upward so that skin caught on the splintered wood. The head lolled against one of the handles, both arms hanging down the sides. He stuffed them in, forcing them to fit in the space; the legs remaining extended, comical.

By now his own legs were shaking. His hands too. He crouched in the sand a moment, looking over the water to the fog of the horizon. He thought it before he said it: "I'm old." As though frightened by the words, he stood up in haste, taking the cracked heels of the man and pushing until the knees buckled the legs into triangles. He positioned the feet so that they balanced on either corner of the barrow. Then he took a second piece of rope and plaited it around and over until feet, knees, arms were all locked in place. The giant body was now trussed and shrunken and deformed.

Despite his precautions, it tipped, twisted, the head nudging Samuel's hands as the wheelbarrow rumbled over the pebbles. The wheel stuck with every rotation, so that soon he began to anticipate jolts and put the wheelbarrow down in advance, clearing the obstacle, observing the damage done to the wheel, before beginning again.

Once the man groaned, and Samuel waited to see if his eyes would open, but they did not. He pushed on through the wet sand of the water-carved alley between the boulders, so narrow that the sides of the wheelbarrow rasped; and one of the man's knees grated against a rough edge and began to bleed.

Then they were out of the tunnel, off the shore almost, with only the steep incline up loose gray sand to halt them. But the wheel caught again. It would not be pushed, and Samuel backed away, ready to give up. He had tried, hadn't he? He had done enough. He would untie the man, bring food and water if he woke, a blanket maybe, and that would be enough.

Yet he came forward, tried turning the wheelbarrow around in the soft sand. He moved backward, pulling it up the path, even though his arms felt as thin as paper, ready to tear. Then the wheel was stuck again and he was back on his knees. He was all sand now. His shoes held it, as did his pockets, his creased hands. He tried once more.

Then came the breath of the headland, a soft breeze

through yellow grasses, and a solid dirt track lined with clusters of small pink flowers and green-thorned weeds. Above them rose the lighthouse.

It had been white once, last plastered in the middle of the previous century, before the colonial government left them to their independence. Now it was flaking, dull, with orange swaths where the metal railing of the gallery had rusted and leaked its age. The gallery encircled the lantern room, though the floor slats were mostly loose or had long since fallen. At those moments when Samuel stood at the base of the tower, looking directly upward, the remaining slats framed the sky above, marking out, at various times and seasons, clouds, stars, sun, and moon. Once a fortnight, if he felt strong enough, he braved the gallery and clung onto whatever was steady as he cleaned the lighthouse windows with a stick and a damp rag. He had done so only a few days before, coming down from the task dizzy, his jaw slack, seeing dark edges wherever he looked. Now, as he glanced up, the windows reflected the cloudless sky, the sharp rays of the noon sun.

Midway up the tower a deep crack had recently doubled in length, spanning the width of the structure. But nothing would be done about it. Just as nothing had been done about the plaster, the railings, the slats, or the radio transmitter.

Around the base grew short scraggly trees, their trunks and branches cast westward by the prevailing wind so that they seemed ever in flight, and Samuel often wondered, before he stepped out of the door in the morning, whether he might find that they had fled after all.

As he neared the walled-off yard, the clucking began, and he moved aside the old trapdoor that he used as a gate, saying good-naturedly, "All right, girls, stop your noise. I'm back now. I'm here."

The chickens, seven of them, rushed toward him in expectation of food.

"No, it's not for you. Go on now, off with you," he said as he pushed the wheelbarrow the final few meters. He pulled it over the single step into the cottage, and dragged it through the small dark entranceway with its clothes-hooks, anoraks, hats, and worn-heeled boots, into the living area.

A chicken followed him inside, the old one with the reddish feathers, that had never quite managed to make friends with the rest. Samuel did not have the energy to shoo her out, though the birds knew well enough that they were not allowed past the threshold. He knelt, letting her come to him and peck at nothings in his hand as he stroked her back. He inspected the bald patches of her breast and thighs, places where she had been attacked. Her wounds had healed. Soon, he hoped, the feathers would return.

"All right now," he said after a while and put her aside.

He untied the ropes. Then he slowly tipped the wheelbarrow over until the man fell out onto the threadbare carpet. Samuel repositioned the limbs, the neck, checked on the knee that was no longer bleeding, took an old cushion and placed it under the man's head. The chicken clucked closer, walking up and down the length of the body.

Samuel went into the kitchen and drank two glasses of water before sitting on a chair at the kitchen table. There were still crumbs from breakfast, and the last remains of a loaf. He baked his own bread twice a week in the old gas oven, having taught himself over the years until he had come up with a recipe with which he was satisfied. He wiped the table down with a broad hand, the crumbs falling into the palm of the other, and coaxed the chicken toward him with little sounds. But she was not interested, preferring to walk around the man on the floor, ruffling her feathers a little.

"Silly thing," he said and, still seated, leaned over to the sink and dropped the crumbs into it. "You'll be sorry later when you're fighting the others for your share of dinner."

But by now the chicken had settled, lying down beside the man's legs, her lids heavy. Samuel looked at the face of the man. A wide mouth in a narrow jaw. He appeared to have no hair on his face at all, not even eyebrows. He might have been in his early thirties, though Samuel would not have been surprised to learn that he was older or younger. Below the earlobe, a little inward, he could make out the pulse at work. Again, he found himself counting. One. Two. Three. Four. Five. Six.

How long might the man live? How long would he lie on Samuel's carpet in Samuel's home? He rattled his fingers on the table, smoothed a hand over his face. Was it to go on like this, then? This incessant movement in his home. This home that had been his alone for more than two decades of solitude. Was it to be this? This breath, this pulse, this youth, this life, taking over the small cottage, seeping into the floor and walls. He began to feel breathless, to gasp his panic.

He tried to reason with himself. The next day the supply boat would come, as it did every fortnight. It would come and he would hand the man over to them. They would have to take him. They had that obligation.

On the floor, as though in mockery of all he was thinking, a vein surfaced on the man's forehead, swollen and quick, ferocious with life.

Samuel stood abruptly, and stumbled out through the door. He would go and fetch the drum. When he returned, he hoped, the man would be dead.

He untied the barrel from his back, placing it in the yard, then took a moment to lean against the stone wall, his legs sinking a little as he did. He thought to sit a while on the cold ground, but raised himself instead, straightening his shoulders. From habit he took the path back toward the cottage, yet at the sight of the open door leading into the dark hall, he stepped away, walking toward the lighthouse, turning his back on the place where that man lay.

The low sun was bright in his face, so that he blinked and put a hand up to cover his tearing eyes. There followed a strange sensation in his ears, of heat and breath, that forced him to turn again and confront the open door.

It had begun to sigh now, the cottage. That must be the feeling in his ears: the doorway sucking in the air of the island, breathing out the stale air of the cottage.

The man was alive. Samuel could think of nothing else. Only of that man's breath. Not of his own frailty and pain, not of his hunger, not even of his desire to be inside, lying on the couch, perhaps to sleep a few moments as his discomfort settled.

But he could not enter that gasping hole. To enter it would be to suffocate, to die.

Inside him something small and folded began to shift. It opened outward, growing ever larger, until his chest, his arms, his throat were wrapped in it. Until he was brittle and creaking with it. He reached up, but could feel only the rasp of fingers on stubble, and beneath it, paper skin.

No, he could not enter the cottage. Nor could he return to the beach, not on these tired legs. And even if he had been able, he would not go. Not now that it had become a place of dread.

The unfolding continued, and he was stretched thin by it, so thin and formless that he might at any moment be taken up by the wind, removed.

In the yard the chickens were clucking for their evening meal. Samuel went around to the side of the cottage where the storage bin for the feed was kept. He lifted the heavy lid and took an enamel mug resting on top of the grain. The mug was army green with a big circle of rust that reached up to the lip and over. Smaller dots of discoloration were in other places—the base, the handle. Samuel dipped it into the grain, feeling the beaded resistance, the increase of weight as the mug filled. His fingers, thick at the best of times, were swollen by the day's toil, and his hand was now that of a giant holding an item from a child's tea set. He scattered the contents, returning twice, thrice to the bin before he was done. The chickens had already advanced, pecking at the dust with such rapidity that they seemed to have forgotten their day of foraging for insects and worms.

His stomach gurgled; he had not eaten since morning. He dipped his hand into the bin and tossed a few grains into his mouth. They tasted of dust, of the wooden bin they were kept in. He no longer had the teeth for chewing such things, but he sucked them, moving them between his cheeks.

While there was still light he ought to gather the eggs. He looked under bushes, in hollows, inside the communal coop, and came out with only three. Among some pebbles he found the remains of one, the shell cracked, streaked with yolk. There was scattered shell on the stone wall, too, and some near the path. He wondered how many more had been lost to the gulls. The little red hen, he knew, wasn't laying any longer. She was too old now and unwell. In the past he would readily have wrung her neck, boiled her, eaten her. He got little enough meat as it was. But each day he felt himself prevented, felt that if only she had more food, more rest, she would improve.

Just then, squabbling broke out among the brood. He turned to see the other hens upon the red one, which had come outside again. They beat their wings, made attacks that caused small feathers to fly up, to hover and drop. Samuel put down the three eggs and went over, inserting his hand into the fray. The plumage of the little red hen was ruffled and there was a spot of blood above her eye, another on her naked breast. She clucked nervously as Samuel removed her, carrying her to a coop he had fashioned a few days previously out of driftwood and fishing net. He stroked her back and brought a pile of grain for her to eat alone, but she sat with her eyes closed, refusing even to be fed by hand.

He rose and walked past the other chickens, their clucking diminishing as they returned to feed. He went through to the rows of the vegetable garden, took a plastic crate that lay propped against the wall, and shook out any spiders or insects that might have made a home in it since the previous evening. He walked along the rows, conscious that he was picking for two, not one.

The vegetables were different from those he had grown up with as a child, different from the crops the family had grown on their piece of land in a valley he remembered as being green and warm. There his parents had shown him how to plant and reap maize, cassava, kale, and how to knock trees in such a manner that mangoes and coconuts fell from them. His sister was just a baby on his mother's back then. Samuel brought her bananas that she sucked on happily, smearing her face.

The garden he had now was more like that of the mission school, the building cluster at the far end of the valley to which he and neighboring boys walked in the mornings, oftentimes rehearsing the Our Father, each boy with his own version of the prayer so that they misled one another until the words became a meaningless jumble, and they were beaten for it.

Each pupil planted, weeded, picked, and ate from the mission school garden. Pumpkins the size of a cow's head, cauliflower and broccoli, strange purple roots that dyed everything pink, even their urine. They would leave the picked vegetables outside the kitchen door, only to receive them again the following day at lunch, transformed into a gray, boiled mash that tasted of nothing.

Now, as he had been taught by his parents and the missionaries, Samuel was careful with his rows, keeping them neat, weeded, never picking more than was necessary. He composted the sandy island soil, spanned nets to protect the plants from the birds the way his father had done with sacking and the missionaries had done with any boy who they felt had not recited his lesson well enough. It was, for a day, that boy's job to act as scarecrow, tolling a hand bell through the rows in a rhythm that was not permitted to waver.

Those days in the valley, the bell's measured tolling, green insects, phrases chanted, and words, the weight of a pumpkin in his arms, a mouth full of food, and that bell, chiming the seconds of growth in the garden. Memories that were now little more than a taste or a scent, too distant to be anything greater.

He filled the metal watering can at the standpipe and went along the rows, bending down afterward to poke a finger in the soil to make sure that the water had seeped in well enough. It was darkening now and he walked the last row slowly, taking his time as he felt the wet soil, and touched the leaves. Rising, he saw the weed. He had named it smotherweed when he first came to the island and found it growing everywhere, climbing the walls of the cottage and tower, carpeting the land all around.

"You can't do anything about it," his predecessor, Joseph, had told him. "It's no good trying to tame the island to your will. It will do as it wants."

But Samuel had had other plans and spent his first year working to clear the smotherweed. Yet every week he found at least one new growth, and here it was again, sitting between two stones on the wall as though it had been invited. He made sure to pull it out with its root before taking it to a scorched slab of cement near the standpipe. There he manipulated the weed with lit matches, watching it twist and shrivel, not stopping until he was certain enough damage had been done that it would never grow again.

The man had not died when Samuel at last reentered the cottage. In fact, he had crawled across the floor and was leaning against the couch, his arms stretched over the seat as though he had been trying to push himself up.

"What are you—?" Samuel began, but his throat was dry and the words would not come. He gathered saliva in his mouth, swallowed, loosened some grain from his cheek, and tried again. "What are you doing?"

The man raised his eyes. The whites were yellow, the pupils unfocused. He spoke a word that Samuel did not understand, or perhaps had not heard correctly. He took a step forward and the man repeated it, holding out his hand as a beggar might do, as Samuel himself had done as a child with his sister when his family had been forced to move to the city. Then in middle age, his hands as arthritic as an old man's from his twenty-three years in prison, he had been sent out begging again. But he had had no child as a prop, no benefit of youth to help him compete with the throngs of young men and women haunting the traffic lights at intersections. Meat on skewers, bananas, fried chicken, stuffed toys, wooden carvings. The lust for acquisition everywhere around him. Always someone hawking, someone buying, and all of it done among the traffic as bone-thin dogs dodged cars in search of refuse.

The man motioned with his hand again, this time bringing it up to his mouth as one might do with a cup. He repeated the word.

"Water?" Samuel asked, and went through to the kitchen. From the cupboard he took an orange-colored plastic mug with a two-holed handle. A mug made for a child's hand. The rim had been chewed, the plastic was flaking, but that was how it had been when he found it washed up on the shore one day. Somebody's unwanted castoff or a beachgoer's loss swept away by a wave.

He filled the cup from the tap and took it through to where the man lay. Though his hands trembled, the man was able to hold the cup, to bring it to his lips. He gulped noisily, spilling onto his chest and his still-damp shorts. The water made him cough and snort. Clear liquid ran from his nostrils down to his lips. He wiped it away and then held out the cup to Samuel, shaking it. He spoke a hoarse word. He wanted more.

Samuel returned to the kitchen, and opened the tap too wide, the water gushing white with force. When he took the cup away it was only half full. He had to do it again, slower, with a trickle that filled the cup to the brim.

Again the man gulped, spilling less this time. When he was done, his hand fell, slender fingers still hooked in the double holes of the handle. Drops splashed onto the carpet. The man closed his eyes, leaned his head back, licked his lips, and swallowed. Then he opened his eyes, one at a time, looked at Samuel, and spoke.

Samuel shook his head. "I don't understand."

The man pushed down against the seat of the couch, trying to lift himself up. He did so without any sound, his face twisted into a bright-toothed grimace. Samuel stood away, watching. He did not want to have that body against his own again. The man raised himself enough to be sitting on the couch.

"Your clothes are wet. You should change. Aren't you cold?"

The man nodded, as though he understood. Then he slid sideways until his head was on the opposite end of the couch, his long torso just fitting, and his eyes closed in sleep.

He had only one sharp knife. It had been large, neatly balanced with a broad wooden handle, but the tip of the blade had snapped off, leaving the knife blunt-nosed. Over time he had sharpened it, but the shape was unusual. Thick-based, tapering to a sudden very thin point. No doubt it would snap again one day.

Samuel took the pot in which he had been soaking beans since the morning. They had grown in size and softened. Skin-halves floated in the water after they had swollen loose. He rinsed the beans at the tap and then looked in the cupboard under the sink for the biggest pot he had. It was right at the back, dusty. He washed it, wiped the lid, and transferred the beans and new water to it before putting it to boil. It was a portion for a single man, carefully measured out. But tonight that portion would have to stretch to two.

He cleaned the vegetables, using his nails to claw off bird droppings where they had fallen. Each vegetable he turned over, seeking holes where worms or insects might have crawled in, and he pursued the trails with the fine point of the knife, tossing his findings into the sink to wash away later. He lifted a wooden chopping board from where it had been leaning against the tap. It smelled of onion, the smell persisting over the years no matter how many times he scrubbed it. The stink of it transferred to his fingers. Some of the vegetables he peeled, all of them he chopped into chunks before separating them into two piles—the hard and the soft. After a time he added the hard to the pot. Then he reached up to the cupboard above the sink for salt and pepper. Both were running low. He emptied them into the pot and stirred with a wooden spoon, before returning the empty cruet to its place. The supply boat would bring more the next day.

Samuel stilled in a moment of irritation. He had forgotten. Forgotten that he had asked them to bring manure. Forgotten to prepare the soil for it. There was no time now, it was dark already. If he woke early enough, he might manage. And he began to divide the garden into manageable sections, slicing the air with his knife as he imagined it.

But no, he would wait. Wait until the man had left, until the island was his again.

On the stove the stew was boiling and Samuel added the soft vegetables to it. He wiped the counter, threw the peelings into a bucket for the chickens, put the seeds aside so that he could plant them again, and washed the knife and board. In the sink one of the worms had managed to crawl to the far end and was now attempting to climb up the side. Samuel splashed some water in its direction, watching it curl up and wash away toward the plug hole where the others had already been lost.

Now the man was at the doorway, dressed in clothes that Samuel had left for him. The jersey was too short, as were the trousers.

"Do you want to eat?" Samuel asked.

The man looked back blankly.

Samuel pointed at his stomach, his mouth, the pot on the stove. "Are you hungry?"

The man smiled. He nodded.

Samuel gestured at the table and chair. Then he went into the living area, returning a moment later with a three-legged stool for himself. It was speckled with paint stains and the long-ago paths of woodworm. He took a trivet from the counter and placed it in the center of the table, gloved his hands in a pot holder, and carried the stew to the trivet.

He paused. He had only one plate. He used it for all his meals; there had never before been a need for another. Though, in truth, there was one more: a gilt-edged cake plate that was on display in the living room despite its chips and cracks. It had come to him in a box of charity items. When he had lifted it out from among the bric-a-brac, he had imagined it once having had a place on the dining room table of the country's first president—whose mansion boasted a hall with a table that could accommodate one hundred guests at a time, all seated under a cascade of glistening crystal chandeliers.

"This is what Africa can be! This is what Africa is!" had been the president's pronouncement, sending out photos for the newspapers to publish, and printing leaflets that were carried through the slums for dispersion to the poor and illiterate. "We are not lost without the colonizers. Look at what we are in our independence!"

The leaflets were black-and-white, and if Samuel had at one time been able to make out the pattern of the dinner service, he could not recall it now. He remembered, though, bringing a leaflet to where his father lay, showing him the message from the president whom he had fought for. "China," his father had called the dinner service, and so when the plate came to Samuel, he associated it with the country of that name, believing the illustration on it to be of that far-off place. But Chimelu, one of the boatmen from the supply ship, whose wife, Edith, worked for a charity and had sent the box, corrected him. "China means the stuff the plate is made from. See, it isn't China at all, it's England." He turned the plate over, showing with his finger as he read, " 'Sutherland China'—that's the thing the plate's made from, like I was saying. 'Made in England.' So there you have it. Just as I said."

The design was blue on a white background. It showed a castle with a tower that reminded him of his lighthouse, without the light.

"That part, the buildings, that would be brown, I guess, in real life," Chimelu said, pointing over Samuel's shoulder. "And then this is a lawn, you know, like grass, only it's short and soft and very green. This in front, that is a lake, and look, there's a little man in a fishing boat, just like you."

"I don't have a boat."

"No, what I mean is he's alone there. He's probably the king. Like you are the king of this place, in your way, you know."

Samuel held the plate and looked at it again. The lake was surrounded by tall, leafy trees, encircled by a floral border.

"I am telling you, it's old this. Probably a valuable antique. Very special," Chimelu said.

"No, it isn't," said John, the other boatman. "Don't give him ideas. It says right there 'Historical Britain Souvenir. Bothwell Castle.' There's probably thousands of them. There's nothing special about it."

"I don't mind," Samuel had replied, and that evening he'd made a wire holder for it so that he could hang it on the wall.

He would not eat from it. Instead he took the small pot in which he had soaked the beans earlier and used that as a bowl. He dished in for each of them, giving the man a long-tined fork with a black plastic handle, himself a tin spoon.

The man ate rapidly, pausing only once to rub his stomach and smile, to show that the food was good.

When he finished he held out his plate for more. Anger rose in Samuel. He had fed him, hadn't he? He had done his duty. Was he meant to feed the man to the point of bursting?

He remembered, then, sitting across from his sister. He had been released from prison, gone to her, and they had been sitting at the table in her kitchen eating dinner, as he was doing with the man. He was chewing when Mary Martha turned to him and said, "Jesus, what's the good of you? You're just another mouth to feed."

He frowned now, where he sat in his own kitchen, frowned at that plate being held out to him. He raised his hands slightly, as though in surrender, indicating that he had had enough. "Help yourself. Eat it all."

The man seemed to understand. He pulled the pot toward himself, tilting it. He spooned food onto the plate, spilling some. These pieces he picked up with his fingers, put them into his mouth. He scraped until the pot was empty, and then lifted the wooden spoon to his mouth, licking it clean. Realizing that he was being watched, he stopped. He spoke, pointing at his body, the length of it, at his stomach. Then he laughed, shook his head. He had made a joke. He returned to the plate, using a finger to slide food onto the fork. After each mouthful he sucked the finger clean. His lips glistened.

Samuel rose, began to wash up. He could not watch any longer.

As he washed the dishes, Samuel looked for a blackened arc on the pot's base. The food had caught, burned at the bottom. He had tasted the bitterness as he ate, and an acrid odor lingered in the room. Yet the pot showed no charring.

Samuel sniffed the air, his face tilted upward. It was certainly there, the smell. Something had burned or was burning. But he could find no source for it. His nose began to itch in preparation for a sneeze, his eyes to water. Revulsion and a rapid anxiety caught him in the stomach, causing him to bring up a little of the meal in his throat and taste the lumpen acidity at the back of his tongue. He swallowed it down, then coughed, afraid to turn around, to move at all. He leaned his weight against the cupboard at his thighs. The scent held him trapped.

From far off, the memory of a man speaking: a young man in a suit, with a mustache, a hat on his lap. This young man was talking to a girl beside him of seventeen or eighteen, talking so loudly that Samuel, three rows away and new to meetings of this sort, had been able to hear every word, so that he was distracted from the speeches he'd come to listen to. The girl's mouth was lipsticked, thin; her ears pierced, with small hoops in them. She skewed her head away from the man, his voice too loud. She was looking around, hardly moving her neck, as though embarrassed and wishing to know who had observed her in this moment. Samuel caught her eye, smiled nervously, and raised his eyebrows comically, while beside her the man continued to talk, ". . . you know why they say that about it?" The girl shook her head to indicate that he should be quiet, but he took it as a sign to carry on.

"They say it—the smell of burning bread—they say it's what you smell right before you die. Yes, that of all the smells in the world is what comes to tell you your time is up! That's how I know this meeting is safe. I smell nothing like that. We won't be raided." He laughed loudly, clutched his hat, laughed again, and two seats away from Samuel, Meria half raised herself from her chair, hissed across the rows, "Can't you shut the fuck up? Some of us are trying to listen."

At the recollection, Samuel's knees folded a little, knocking against the cupboard door. It was happening then. He was about to die. Now at the age of seventy, with a stranger on his island, with everything in disarray, the scent of burning had come for him. The smell increased around him, grew thick and suffocating.

He was a boy again, in the green valley, except that it

was no longer green. Orange and black with flame, the subsistence plantations and crops of each individual home were being destroyed. Uniformed men stalked dirt roads with rifles and firebrands, setting alight anything that had been planted or built. Homes, fences, washing lines were aflame, as were chickens that a few of the men kicked between them with their heavily booted feet, cursing with laughter at the game. Others had blades, machetes, any number of sharp objects with which they slit the throats of the livestock. Goats panted blood, cows fell to their knees and then toppled over onto one another. Somewhere a donkey brayed and brayed and brayed, until the sound was put to an end.

They ran. Flame and ash pursued them. From a house ahead of them an old lady stumbled out, waving her thin arms. "Help me! My house is on fire, help me!"

Samuel's father did not stop, did not look in her direction. His mother called, "Grandmother, you must leave. Leave now. Follow us. Run if you can."

But the woman wailed toward the nearest person, clutched onto the man's beige shirt, tugged at his sleeve, his rifle-holding hand. She was tiny, only coming up to his elbow. "Help me," she said. "Help me, help me, help me."

By then Samuel's family was beyond her, but when he looked back she was on the ground, the center of her face bloodied. Even as he fled, he could see her jaw clicking, her eyes skyward.

Their eviction had been spoken flatly by a translator

with an accent they did not recognize. The arable valley was now the property of the colonists. "You are to return to the mountains where monkeys belong, by order of the governor. The land is no longer yours. Glory to the King and glory to the great Empire."

At first no one had believed the man's words. Who could make them move, they who had been here for generations further back than they could count? But then the men came and they were shown that no one would be allowed to remain. The land had been taken.

They fled with nothing, never stopping. Not even when his mother tripped, his sister, tied to her back, knocking her head so hard that a bump rose immediately. She had been crying, now she screamed. Yet still they ran, amid their own blood and spittle, as the black cloud of the burning valley hunted them, chasing them forward, forward, toward the blue sky.

Those fleeing ahead of them had stripped bare land and villages as they came to them. Destructive as locusts, they harvested whatever they could, leaving in their wake stalks, bones, robbed nests, a trail of hunger unsated.

Most took without asking, and there were many who used force. They broke into houses, made threats, committed murder. Groups came together in villages and used their numbers to loot general stores, fleeing with sacks of meal and beans. Those who came afterward scratched through the detritus for whatever could be found. A handful of groundnuts, a moldering sweet potato. But not Samuel's family. His father forbade it. "What was ours has been stolen," he said. "How can we, who know what it is to be robbed of everything, behave in the same way toward someone else?"

"The food is there, Father, and we're hungry," Samuel replied.

"Is that what you have to say to me? Haven't I taught you—didn't the missionaries teach you—to do unto others as you would have them do unto you? Remember, God is watching you always. He can see a crime, no matter how high up in heaven he is."

"But only a banana from a tree. Only that. For us to share."

His father ignored him, moving forward as though his ankles were hobbled; his left foot so blistered that he could walk on the edge of the heel alone.

By nightfall they sat a little way from the roadside, under a tree. Samuel listened irritably to the suckling of his sister at his mother's breast. The bump on her head was a hard protuberance, an almost iridescent red. Beside her sat his father with closed eyes and clasped hands, whispering a continuous prayer. The ground was damp. The baby suckled. His father murmured. Samuel's hunger gnawed at him, biting and powerful as if done by the mouth of God himself.

In the kitchen, the memory of burning had driven away the scent. It was food that he could smell now. He placed the washed pot on the sideboard to dry. The sharpness of onion was on his hands, at his feet peelings curled in the bucket. From behind him came the sound of chewing, of licking. He softened a little, and turned to face the man, to watch the plate being wiped clean with a finger. If, on that day when the valley burned, someone had offered him a plate of food, he, too, would have been inclined to hold it out and ask for more. He could not blame a fleeing man for his hunger.

The toilet was outside the cottage, round the back. At one time it would have been more easily accessible, no less than ten steps from a back door in the kitchen. But a predecessor had bricked up the doorway from the inside, so that the door itself was visible outside only, handleless, with a wad of ancient paper in the rusted keyhole; the windows, with most of the panes missing, showed through to thick cement and badly chipped bricks in tilted rows.

Samuel showed the man where the heavy black torch hung in the hallway and then, switching it on, led the way past the tower to the outhouse. The door was short, leaving wrist-sized gaps at the bottom and top. They gave some ventilation and light in the windowless structure—though Samuel rarely took the trouble to close the door while inside.

The floor of the outhouse was slightly sunken, and Samuel touched the man on his shoulder, showing with the torch to warn of the step down. Because of the drop, there was flooding in rainy weather, so Samuel had placed two bricks on the floor, a leg width apart. The room was small; he had to squeeze past the man and push him into the open door as he put his feet on the bricks, crouching a little to show what they were for.

The man frowned.

Samuel waved a hand in dismissal, shook his head. It wasn't going to rain that night. It didn't matter.

The bricks were the type with three holes in the center, and spiders lived inside those holes, as they did behind the door and in the corners. Cobwebs hung thick and gray from the ceiling. The man, tall as he was, brushed them away from his head, ducking a little.

Samuel pointed out where two rolls of toilet paper stood atop an upturned log. It was thin paper, the cheapest kind, lightly textured with small bumps. Samuel tore a piece off, pointed at the toilet bowl, shook his head again, and said, "No, no, no," then tossed the wadded ball into a lidded bin on the other side of the toilet. Once a week the paper was burned. He looked around now for what else there might be to mention, his arm pressed against the wall. He could feel the bubbling plaster popping under his weight, bits snagging at his jersey. He said, "Ah," and indicated that the man should swap places with him. On the left side of the toilet hung a chain flush mechanism attached to a cistern high up on the wall. At one time the chain had snapped a link, and Samuel had repaired it with wire. He pointed out the suture to the man as a courtesy. It was too high for Samuel to reach, but the tall man might do so accidentally and puncture his hand on the sharp points. Samuel pulled on the ring at the bottom of the chain, jerking hard twice before the room was alive with the loud flushing. Both men looked into the bowl, dark with a day's urine, watching it fill and release with rainwater collected in a metal tank on the roof. The waste went down tunnels that Samuel had dug himself—years they had taken him to mine in the hard earth, years of labor so that his shit could flow into the sea. He did not know how to tell the man to flush sparingly, that it should only be done once a day, and so he did not try.

There was no basin. Samuel led the man round to the outside tap where a pouch made from a rag hung on the spout. Inside the rag were scraps of soap. He showed the man how to wet the pouch, to rub it between his hands until it foamed, and then to wash his face and hands and neck. A proper wash with a plastic basin and stove-warmed water wasn't necessary. Let the washing of the man be someone else's responsibility.

Nor did he have a toothbrush and toothpaste. They were not things he had grown up with. Instead he used a finger and ash or twigs chewed to a soft, wide tip. Toothpaste he had experienced for the first time in middle age when he left prison and went to live with his sister. His sixteen-year-old niece had held her nose with her green-painted nails, complaining that he stank, that his teeth were coffee-colored.

"Didn't you look after yourself in prison?" Mary Martha asked.

"They didn't give us toiletries. Our clothes were washed sometimes, but the rest we were supposed to buy or get from family or friends."

"So it's my fault, is it? I had a family, if you remember. I had our parents—with Daddy the way he was— and two children to look after on my own. Do you see a husband here? No, because there isn't one. There never was. And, you'll notice, I'm not even mentioning Lesi. I am not even mentioning that I had to take in your child when both his parents were criminals. Who else would have done that? Who else? Not any of your meeting friends and comrades. Not any of them. It was me. That's who took him in. And you sit there complaining about toothpaste."

"No, sister, I'm not complaining. You've done enough."

And later, when he had come from the bathroom holding his throat, asking, "Is it meant to burn like this?" she had said, "Oh for heaven's sake, did you swallow it? Even Daddy learned how to brush his teeth. Even he could do it."

Samuel left the man in the outhouse and walked to the front of the yard. The night was clear, heavy with stars, and he could easily make out the white tower of the lighthouse. Always at night it looked its best, this tower that seemed squat and ravaged by the elements in the waking hours, was tall, even majestic now, its plaster bright. From its summit the beam extended out, away from the island, passing over the still, black ocean, stroking the dark rock half a mile out where seabirds slept.

The beam of light came one-two-pause-one-two-pause. A signal that pulsed out over the island and ocean, while across the bay a red light shone at the mainland harbor, and beyond it a hundred thousand glowing punctures marked the city. A city that seemed afloat in the black sea, drifting, drifting, going nowhere.

He heard the man coughing inside the outhouse and wondered how long he might still be in there. A chill wind was blowing, its whistle and howl loud where it met with window gaps or struggled through tree branches. Samuel walked over to the tree that neighbored the tower and kept his head low, his body close to the trunk as he urinated.

The pulsing beam continued. But Samuel was uneasy. The pause between the pulses was too long. Not by much. Half a second. A second. Like a heart rate slowing down. Perhaps the mechanism needed oiling. He took a step toward the lighthouse door, and as he did the wind whipped at him, blowing his jacket up around the back of his head. He pulled it down and trotted heavily back to the cottage. He would go and fix the mechanism tomorrow. Today he was too tired. His body ached. He could not think of making it up the tower stairs. Tomorrow. Tomorrow.

It was early yet. No more than seven or half past. He

sat on the couch, leaned his head back with a sigh. There was something soft against his neck, something unfamiliar. He reached behind him and brought forward the man's shorts. They had been left there, on the couch back, in a heap. They were dark, or had been at one time, faded now to the color of charcoal, decorated with patches of salt stain.

Samuel wanted to throw them in the kitchen bin. Burn them on the next disposal day. Instead he got up heavily, took a bucket from the kitchen corner, and half filled it with water. From a cupboard where he kept his cleaning materials, he took a box of cold water washing powder, the top corner torn open. He chucked some into the bucket, splashed with his hand until suds formed. He pushed the shorts in, they billowed and then floated. Down he pushed again, over and over, one handed, as the suds grew up his arm and the shorts washed the water gray.

When he believed all the salt to have been dissolved and the sand to have been released, Samuel emptied the dirty water into the sink and rinsed the shorts in clean water. It was too windy to hang them outside so he wrung them out as best he could and hung them on a nail in the wall, placing the bucket beneath to catch the drops.

The man came inside and returned the torch to its hook in the hallway, then went into the lounge, clasping his hands together, blowing on them. Water glistened in his hair. He took the blanket that Samuel offered him and wrapped it around his shoulders, wearing it like a cape. Then he went and sat on one half of the couch, shivering as Samuel boiled water and made tea for them.

They sat side by side awkwardly, blowing, sipping, blowing. After a while Samuel got up, went to the television set, and switched it on. It buzzed and squealed, the screen gray, before he turned it off again.

"It's not working," he said. "Sorry."

At times he would put on a video in the evening, for company, while he mended clothes with large, clumsy stitches, or fiddled with his toolbox and some or other thing that needed repairing.

The man half raised himself on the couch, as though he felt it was expected of him. He watched Samuel, waiting, and when Samuel picked up a few old magazines from the shelves, holding them out, he shook his head and sat back down.

Samuel returned the magazines to their place. "Nothing worth seeing in them anyway."

The man continued to sip his tea.

"Chimelu—you'll meet him tomorrow when he comes with the supply boat—his wife sends them to me. Sends me what the charity shop can't sell. No one wants videos anymore, not nowadays, or old magazines like these."

The man put down his mug on the coffee table and wrapped the blanket tighter around his body.

Samuel coughed, waved a hand at the shelves, touched the spines of some of the videotapes. He began to say something, but instead picked up a magazine and turned it over so that the cover was no longer visible. They dismayed him, these movies and magazines from his country. The people in them seemed to him as foreign as the man on his couch. Sunglassed, tattooed, clad in silk and gold jewelry, they spoke a language reduced to crudities and slang, all oaths and stumblings. They were stiff as mannequins, each trying to emulate something far out of their reach. The films showed lovers, dance clubs, drugs and traffickers, as though that were all of it, everything. As though there were no history, and all the past was something that had happened elsewhere, to be remembered by others.

Yet he knew something about the allure of bounty and shine. Of what it had done to him, arriving in the city to see the suited men, hair altered by pomade. From the street corner where he begged, he watched them walking, standing in line at the bus stop. They talked loudly, tilted their hats at one another. Or, if alone, made a show of reading the newspaper, huffing, shaking their heads, turning the pages and folding them noisily until the paper was a manageable size. In the slum where they lived, there were women with wigs and cheap satin dresses, women who, in exchange for gifts of stockings and clip-on earrings, allowed themselves to be taken into alleyways and pressed up against walls. Those things had seemed meaningful to Samuel. Those were the things that began to matter, and he found himself embarrassed by his father's praying, and by his mother's naked face, her country clothes, her hair in scruffy braids against her scalp.

That other world had vanished behind them, and here in the city, at the gray intersection where he begged alongside his sister and a blind lady known as Mama Blue, he watched people passing, bright and glimmering, against a background dull as newsprint. Vast cars drove by carrying white-suited men, their pale wives holding handkerchiefs to their noses—men who had been sent by the crown to rule and enforce order. Their cars were accompanied by guards on motorcycles. When they weren't riding, these guards followed their madams and bosses, carrying parcels, nudging people out of the way, swearing at the beggars who tried to follow.

Children ran among the bus queues; they were native-born, displaced or orphaned in various ways by the colonizers. They picked pockets, filched from street vendors, and stooped to gather the still-smoldering butts of cigarettes. Samuel observed them as another child might the pictures in a children's book. He considered how it would be to step out of the dust and exhaust fumes, to walk into the pages of their color and noise. How he would adopt their fearlessness, instead of the tentative knocks he gave on car windows, his hand held out for change. How he would be something more than the boy who received half-eaten apples and shared them with his little sister and the toothless lady who raised her milk-blue eyes up to the sky and augured rain or hunger or failure for the day to come.

In the quiet of a midmorning, one of the boys, the one they called Dog, whistled across from the bus station. He and his friends had managed to steal an entire sack of oranges from an unattended delivery truck. They were cutting open the sack with a pocket knife, and had begun to share out the spoils. Dog saw Samuel watching them, whistled, said, "Come here."

Samuel didn't move.

"Come here. We want to talk to you."

Samuel crossed the street and stood in front of the boys in silence.

"Have you ever had one of these before?" asked Dog, holding up an orange.

Samuel shook his head.

"Then today you're lucky because I'm going to give you one. See, you take off the skin like this." He bit into it and pulled a piece off with his teeth before proceeding to peel it with his fingers. "Give him one, Laps."

A boy whose face and hands were dripping with juice threw one for Samuel to catch. But Samuel missed. The orange rolled away, off the pavement, into the gutter. The boys sniggered as Samuel turned to pick it up and crossed back to his sister.

First he held it to his nose. The smell was sharp. He let his sister sniff it and then told her to pass it on to Mama Blue. She smelled it for a long time before handing it back.

"What is it?" she asked.

"It's called an orange. That's what he said."

"Who said?"

"One of those beggar boys."

"Oh, well, then you can be sure it isn't true. Those street boys know nothing. They've never even been to school."

"Did you go to school?"

"Not me. There was no school when I was a child."

Mary Martha tugged at his arm. "Are we going to eat it?"

He bit the flesh as he had seen Dog do. It was bitter, horrible. He looked back at the boys to see if they were watching him and laughing. But they were lying on their backs, orange skins all around them. He began to peel it slowly, the rind blowing out a fine spray over his hands. Inside were segments. He divided them into three parts, putting first one into each proffered mouth. It was golden to taste. A feast. Golden and wet. He wished he had the courage to ask for more.

A few days later Dog called to Samuel again.

"Come here, boy. We want to talk to you."

Samuel said, "Wait here" to Mary Martha, before crossing the street.

"We're going to the cinema on Albert Street. Are you coming?"

"I have no money. I can't."

"Do you think we have money?" Dog laughed. "We sneak in."

"What about my sister?"

"She's too young. Leave her with Mama Blue. A

blind lady with a little girl will make more money than a blind lady alone."

The film had been a gangster movie from America. Though it was in black and white, it was like the pages of the book he had been observing come to brilliant and startling life. Afterward, Samuel imitated the accents, remembered the lines, reenacted certain scenes for the boys. In the public park, he stole the hat off a man sleeping on a bench, swaggered, peered out from under the brim. He feigned a gun in his pocket, shooting his finger at each boy in turn, as though they were his enemies. He was given the nickname American and was called on to repeat the performance for other boys who had not been with them.

Loitering became his daily habit. He abandoned his sister to begging, bribing her with stolen sweets not to tell their parents that he left her alone all day so that he could play at thieving and wealth with boys who had no homes.

I n the city, days emerged already soiled. Immense heat, a sky of murk, traffic that never slowed or lessened.

Samuel's parents walked the streets in search of jobs or piecework that rarely came. Sometimes they begged outside grocery stores or in the maw of the bazaar. At the worst times his father stood humiliated outside the church, a hand out in supplication. He bobbed his head when strangers gave coins, afterward clutching them in a fist so that they made no sound as he entered the building and prayed.

There was a day when he left the church with nothing, and he could not turn as he should, could not take the path back home. Instead he went elsewhere, walking without aim through the burning gray of the day's setting sun, until his attention was caught by a group of men outside a house on the other side of the street. There were at least forty of them, talking in low tones, their gestures forceful. Samuel's father joined them as they began to enter the house, making his way through a small hallway into the front room. Age stains on the walls and floor showed where furniture had recently been moved away to make more space. Already the floor was full of seated men, their knees pulled up to their chests. He sat down beside a man in the uniform of a house boy. In front of him was a man in a suit, another in the clothes of a butcher, the smell of soap and fat coming from him.

That first meeting was something he often spoke of afterward. He was a quiet man, but for his remaining years he regularly described it as though it were something miraculous, as though it were some kind of regeneration.

"I didn't know what it was about," he would begin, "that first time at the house, I didn't know. I didn't understand what they were saying. I heard the words, but what could they mean to me as I was? But I stayed and I listened. They talked, and the more they talked, well, it's difficult to describe. I felt something. Something here and here." He pointed at his throat, his hands. "I knew they were right, what they were saying. I knew it. There's no more to it than that."

The next afternoon he returned. The front door was closed. He knocked and listened as someone sighed, and then the sigh turned into footsteps approaching across the wooden floor. The door was opened by a young man. He wore round spectacles and pushed them up on his nose as he said, "Can I help you?"

Samuel's father looked past him into the front room. The furniture had all been returned. Two wooden benches with cushions. Four chairs, several stools. A cabinet.

"Is there no meeting today?" he asked.

"No, not today. Only Wednesday and Saturday evenings."

Another, older, man entered the front room through a farther door. He was reading a book, his head down. Samuel's father recognized him as the meeting leader.

"Was there anything else?" the young man said.

At the sound of his voice the older man looked up from his book and saw Samuel's father. He smiled. "Is there something you need?"

"He wanted to know about the meetings," the young man said.

"I came yesterday."

"And you hoped there would be another one today?"

"Yes."

"Well, there's no reason why there can't be. You and I can have our own meeting. Come in, please. Will you have coffee? I'm interested in hearing your thoughts."

Samuel's father hesitated, but then the man did something unexpected. He put the book aside, pages downward, on the cabinet. "Just like that," he would always mime in the retelling. "You see, he put the book down for me. Just like that, like it didn't matter at all that he was busy. It was like he believed I was more interesting."

Over the years he returned always to the first visit

and to the second, telling in detail each moment up until the book was cast aside and he entered the house. But of the conversation that followed, of what might have happened during that visit, he never spoke.

The coming Saturday's meeting replaced prayer and begging. He spoke of little else. Yet when the time came to leave, Samuel's father dawdled in the family's one-room home. He smoothed his clothes, complained to his wife about invisible grease stains. He held his forehead, saying he had not slept well because of Friday night drunks in the street. When his daughter brought the cup of coffee that he had asked for, he pushed it away. "Can't you see I'm on my way out? I don't have time to drink that now."

Still he did not leave. He stood at the mirror fragment that hung on the wall between two nails and looked into it, turning his face sideways, up and down. He did not like what he saw. His face was dull. He tried a few expressions—raised eyebrows, a frown, pursed lips.

Samuel was at home. He was sixteen years old and had a hangover that had kept him indoors all day, refusing food. But he said, "Do you want me to go with you?"

"Look at this boy! Waiting until I have one foot out the door before he decides he wants to come. I can't wait for you. I'm leaving right now, so if you're coming, you come now. I don't want to be late." But he waited while Samuel dressed and washed his face.

As it was, they were on time. Samuel's father had walked the entire way at a speed that left Samuel heaving in the gutters and caused a cold line of sweat to form at the back of his neck. He followed his father into the cramped room, thick with breath and heat. The two of them leaned against a wall, his father nodding greetings at the people around them. The wall smelled of greasy hair. Samuel turned his neck a little, then closed his eyes, wishing away the throbbing in his head. He did not pay attention when the speaking began, though he noticed the room's hushing, his father's intake of air. But then the boom of words was at his face, and mutterings neighbored him.

"It's happening in other countries," someone was saying. "Why can't we have our independence too?"

Samuel rolled his eyes. He had heard all of this before in whispered conversations at bus stops or between stall-holders and customers in the market. And once, in the park, idling on a bench, he had heard two passing men. One of them was leaning on a walking stick. "I wasn't anything other than a member of my own tribe," he said. "Then came 1934 and we are told we are all—the whole region, you understand—we're all the same tribe, given the same name. I have nothing against the other tribes, you understand. They're nice people, good people. We have no hatred between us, but they're not my tribe. They're from different areas. So the map says who we are and where we are, but nobody ever asked us if it was right."

"Did you see the map?" the other man asked.

"Oh yes. Someone showed it to me. It was just words and lines. Nothing you could use to find your way anywhere."

Beside Samuel, his father was shivering and had moved forward a little so that a gap now formed between himself and the wall. He was listening intently, his feet and hands tapping, lips moving in the repetition of a single word. Samuel closed his eyes again and dozed where he stood.

Later he woke. His neck hurt. He rubbed it with a cramped movement, watching as a man with a small triangular beard began talking. "At school, and in the churches, the missionaries teach us that the meek will inherit the earth. We have been meek, all of us, and what has our meekness brought us? We have lost our land and ourselves. With meekness we accepted the West, took on all its values and ideals. So much so that we have grown to be ashamed of our own people. That is what the meek have inherited—shame!"

The word meant little to Samuel. What did he have to be ashamed of? He was the American. He could steal or bargain for whatever his family needed. He had friends, admirers, women when he wanted them. All things were good. Perhaps he wished his parents had adapted better to city life, with their clothes and ways that embarrassed him. Was that shame?

But once he had come here, to the island, with the donated videos and magazines, he had begun to understand the man's speech. He saw shame in these men and women on the covers, in the trite story lines and sparkling clothes of the films. Was this what his father had been shivering for when he joined the Independence Movement? Was this the clean slate they'd spoken of when at last the Movement was successful and the colonizers had left?

By then a cripple, his father had reveled in the victory. Though the colonizers had left nothing, destroying what could not be carried—desks, chairs, lightbulbs, medicines, telephones—his father had not seen the destruction as an act of pettiness or violence. His large head and thin body lolled in a chair that Samuel carried out into the street, and he shook the hands of passersby, saying, "It's a new beginning. It happens now."

Overhead airplanes flew for days, their passengers fleeing the country's independence. Already, in the capital, the president-elect had ordered a statue and a fountain, was drawing up plans for his new home. While down below, in the rubble, people were scrabbling as they had always done.

The Second Day

Stiffness held his body when he woke, and he got out of bed with difficulty. His arms, his wrists, and shoulders hurt; his back was concrete, his thighs hardened to stone. Twice he was unable to push himself up off the edge of the low bed. When he was standing at last, it had cost him so much energy that he had none left to raise his head. He simply stood for a minute looking down at his feet. His toenails were thick and dark. Some were long, having become impossible to cut.

On warmer nights Samuel might go barefoot in the cottage, sitting on the couch with one foot positioned in such a way that he could reach it. He would pick at the nails, worrying them until they ripped a little and he could tear them shorter. The skin oftentimes bled where he tore too low. Toes got infected as the nails grew back into the skin, swelling with pus. He hobbled on those days, aware each time his boots pressed against the pain.

This morning he had three ingrown toenails. Both big toes and the middle one on the right foot. He would need to soak his feet in salted water. Warm was best, but the thought of the preparation tired him: the kettle to be filled, the lighting of a match and then of the stove, the basin to be fetched. With that man watching it all. No, it was too much. He would walk down to the beach instead, put his feet in the icy water, and stand there until the cold numbed the pain. But even that seemed like too much trouble. Removing shoes and socks, rolling up his trousers. Then the reverse afterward, with no chair at hand to make it easier.

He pulled off the mismatched tracksuit in which he slept and shuffled across to the wardrobe, feeling for his clothes in the semidark. First he put on a T-shirt and jersey. Underwear, trousers, and socks he carried to the bed, putting them on while seated. He struggled, his fingers thick and clumsy. When he had the last sock pulled up to his calf, he allowed himself to slide back down onto the still-warm sheets. His cheek touched them and he sighed, falling asleep in that moment, his feet raised slightly above the ground.

When he woke again, the day was still only a gray promise at the window. Outside he could hear the chickens stirring. They needed to be fed. Samuel rose with less difficulty than before, though he remained stiff and in pain. It had been years since he had ached like this. Perhaps not since the ride at the back of the prison truck. Some fifty of them being transported from cells in the town center where they had been kept for a week, to the new maximum security prison on what were then still the outskirts of the city.

They came with their torn clothes, their bloodstains, bruises, and swollen eyes. They were rank with sweat, with a week's piss and shit. Over it all was spread the odor of decay. Wounds suppurated and gums had become fleshy arcs, with shards in places where teeth had been. That interminable journey, and the foul hiss of breath as their bodies smashed against one another on the uneven road.

The new prison was vast. So vast that it had been given the nickname the Palace while it was little more than foundations. People guessed at its eventual size, the many corridors and rooms that it would contain. But soon high walls and steel gates were erected. No one approached the walls, or thought to scale them to look over the top and see the progress being made. That would have been a foolish act. It was known, without the need for it to be said, that the prison was being built by order of the Dictator. Within its walls he wished to house his naysayers, his enemies, anyone whom he cared to name as irksome.

Samuel did his best to walk quietly through the living room. His knees cracked with every step. The room smelled foreign after a night of someone else's breath, someone else's body. The man was on the couch, curled up as small as he could go. His breathing was deep, even.

When he reached the hallway, Samuel stifled a groan as he bent for his shoes. Normally he would lace them while seated on the couch, but that was not possible now. He opened the front door, felt the cold of the morning on his face, the first scents of foliage, of salt and wet, then he trod in socked feet across the grainy earth to the steps leading up to the lighthouse door. There were three, and he sat on the middle one, brushing the bottom of each sock with a heavy hand. He laced up his shoes and began to make his way to the yard, his footsteps muffled by the gray waves breaking on the shore.

The chickens greeted him with their usual noise. He

went to the feed bin and scattered grain for them, taking care to give some to the old hen that was still in her makeshift cage. She clucked dolefully as he stroked her and spoke gentle words to soothe her. Afterward he let her out, watching as she went to a bush and sat beneath it, unwilling to go farther.

Samuel followed the rest of the flock to where they were scropping in the vegetable garden. He would not pick anything now. He would wait until the man was gone, do it at his leisure, have a good lunch, perhaps followed by a nap. That was what he wanted. To sleep. To be alone and to sleep.

When he came to the end of the garden, he leaned on the dry-stone wall, feeling the stones grate together under his weight. Below, the sea was restless. White cones foamed and shivered, while on the bouldered shore the foam collected and browned. Nearby, the jetty was a line of darkness on which a tern hunched against the wind. Inland, a portion of the blue-gray wall that passed around the island's perimeter had collapsed in a weak spot. Some of the stones had rolled down, were black with water. The rest had buckled into a heap that leaked out of the neat line. Samuel shook his head. He would be carrying rocks today, breaking others in order to fix the gap. There would be no sleep.

He went back to the cottage and collected the sledge-hammer from where it leaned inside the doorway. His arms throbbed with the weight of it, and he felt the burden of age upon him. Memories were there, too, coming fast that morning—things best forgotten now approaching as steadily as waves approach the shore.

That first day at the Palace. The difficulty of climbing down from the truck as guards shouted, watching as they stumbled and blinked in the bright daylight of the prison courtyard. Topiary trees stood in pots on either side of a doorway. A man came out, uniformed in beige, a military beret on his head. He had sweat marks under his armpits, more sweat on his brow and lip.

"Christ, Sergeant, get someone to fix my ceiling fan. It's stifling in there." Then he called to the corporals in charge of the prisoners and said, "Take them to the yard for now. Anyone die along the way?"

Two soldiers checked inside the back of the truck. "No, Colonel."

The colonel aired his face with a document he was holding, said again that the fan needed fixing, and watched the prisoners being led into a wide windowless corridor. It was unpainted, so new that cement crumbs sounded underfoot. Lights flickered overhead, long and fluorescent, every second or third one threatening to go out. At the end of the corridor they went through an iron-barred gate, large as something from an ancient keep, and stepped into a massive yard.

Across the length of the yard, piles of gray rocks stood at intervals. Each pile was allocated to a group of men. With sledgehammers they broke the rocks into gravel, their legs chained so that they couldn't run.

Though where they might run to wasn't clear, not with high walls topped by armed guards on all sides.

Entering the yard, Samuel had felt his ears shrink at the sound of metal on rock. Still, he craned his neck, made himself taller by leaning forward on his toes. As far as he could see there were only men in the yard. The women must be elsewhere. He was not certain that Meria had been caught—perhaps she had escaped, perhaps she had been sent elsewhere. Even so, she had been forced to be with him in the room of his torture, made to sit beside him by the threats of his captors.

"We will kill your wife," they said.

"She's not my wife."

"The mother of your child, the woman you live with. What do you call that if it isn't a wife?"

"A comrade."

The man with a face marked by acne scars slapped him. "Comrade, wife, whore. It's all the same."

Samuel shrugged himself upright in the chair that he was tied to. He tasted blood. Only a little, but enough to terrify him. And Meria was with him in his fear. He remembered then, in that moment when all else seemed to have faded from him, the sound of her laughter. A little chuckle one of the first times he had spoken to her. He had still had the exaggerated *r*'s, the long vowels of someone trying to sound American.

"Listen to yourself," she'd said. "You're a child. Why do you want to sound like that?" Then she had turned away, giving him the back of her head, her hair shaved down so short that he could see her scalp.

Again, months later when they had slept together for the first time. Her hand patted his shoulder. "You can get off now." She lit a cigarette and puffed out. "Oh, little boy, you fuck like a virgin."

That was what capture brought to him. It did not come with a sense of honor as he had been told it would, it did not come with pride. It brought only memories of humiliations, and a feeling that it would all continue as it had. That all the past and all the future were here in this piss-drenched seat, from which he could not escape.

When they approached him again, made to hit him, he called out, told them what they wanted to know, gave them names and places, fabricating if he had no answer.

The scarred man smirked. "Is this a man? The Dictator will laugh when he hears that this thing is meant to be his enemy."

Samuel sniffed, wiped a sleeve across his top lip. The morning had cooled further with an icy wind coming in from the south. He closed his eyes against it. The waking feeling of exhaustion was with him still; the sledgehammer heavy in his arms. He let it drop slowly, feeling the crunch as the head landed on sand. For a moment he was surprised. He opened his eyes, looked down, and toed the loose sand. In the prison yard the earth had been packed close by labor. It caused sledgehammers to bounce a little if they hit it, sent tremors up prisoners' arms. Samuel clutched the handle now as though he might find in it those distant vibrations. But no, the wood was still. It was only his body's heaviness that was remembering.

The weariness grew in him like a thing coming to life. A thing crawling through him and taking over his body. He could feel it in his eyes, see it almost—a shadow, something dark in the corner of his vision. He blinked, turned, sought to catch it. The handle slipped from him and fell to the ground. Samuel stumbled, then looked up. He had found it, had caught the shadow. It darkened the cottage doorway, moved a little, came forward. Samuel blinked again. It was the man, coming toward him.

The man smiled when he saw Samuel, raising a hand unnecessarily high in a wave. Samuel returned the gesture, his low, at level with his belly. He murmured "Good morning," though the man could not have heard it at that distance.

When he reached Samuel, the man smiled again, pointed at the sledgehammer, and mimed the act of using it. Then he wiped invisible sweat from his brow, puffed elaborately, seeming to suggest that it was hard work.

"Yes," he replied and wiped his own brow in agreement.

The man surveyed the morning. Then, exaggerated as before, he lifted his shoulders, inhaled deeply, and puffed out contentedly. He gestured at the view and made a sign with his hand that seemed to mean something like *good* or *beautiful*.

For a minute the men stood in silence. Samuel cleared his throat, put a toe against the head of the sledgehammer. The man looked around and then wrapped his arms around himself, vibrated his lips, made his body shiver.

"There are jackets in the hallway," Samuel said. "Just take whichever one you can fit into." The man looked at Samuel. "I suppose I'll have to show you."

Samuel took a step back in the direction of the cottage. But the man prevented him from going farther. He placed his hand on Samuel's chest. Samuel felt his heartbeat quicken. The man was very close. He could smell his breath, see the cracks in the dry skin of his lips, the wide pores that dotted his nose. The man held him where he was, and spoke.

"I don't know what you want," Samuel said. "What are you saying? What do you want?"

The man laughed, showing his teeth, big and white. He removed his hand from Samuel's chest, used it to point at his own, then slapped his heart with an open palm as he spoke a word. He repeated it twice, slowly, each time slapping his chest. He took care to enunciate the sounds, guttural, foreign, so that in its exaggerated way it became like a performance, someone growling for a child's amusement.

Samuel exhaled. He understood. It was a name. The man's name. He tried to reproduce it. "Nnn . . . ," he said.

The man made the first sound again.

"Nnnngh?"

The man repeated the word, nodding for Samuel to continue.

"Ngsch . . ." but Samuel could not adapt his mouth to it. He shook his head, waved his hand in the air as though to clear it of the noise he had made.

The man lifted a finger, bent down to write with it in the sand.

"It won't help," Samuel said. "I can't read. I could once, just a little. But that's a long time ago now. I don't remember any of it anymore." Then he pointed at himself, spoke his name, and the man smiled.

"Sang-wool," he said. "Sang-wool."

Samuel nodded. The man gripped his shoulder and smiled again. "Sang-wool."

Then there came the sound of a motor. They looked toward the sea and spotted the supply boat in the distance, slowly approaching from the mainland.

The man tightened his grip on Samuel's shoulder.

"No, don't be afraid. They'll save you. They'll look after you. They're going to take you somewhere safe and give you proper food and clothes. You can't stay here."

"Sang-wool," the man said. His voice was low. He shook his head. He was wild with fright now, his eyes rolling. He brought his hands together, lowered himself to his knees. He looked up at Samuel. "Elp," he said. "Elp, elp elp," until Samuel could no longer deny that the man had spoken *help*. Somewhere he had heard that word, somewhere he had learned it, turning to it now in desperation. In the man's supplication, in his begging use of the word, Samuel recognized his own fear; the fear that he had carried with him for so many years. In prison, and before, and still later, afterward, once he'd been released. The fear that he would die.

"So, come then, come on, come with me, hurry now."

He led the man up the three stone steps of the lighthouse, opened the heavy door and pushed him through into the cold, dimly lit interior. He pointed at the stairwell, "Go up, up!" The man stumbled on the first stair, moved forward on hands and knees. Samuel shut the door, turned the key in the lock. The key resisted, grinding stiffly as he forced it. Rust grimed his fingers. His mouth felt dry. He blinked the shadow back into the corners of his eyes and walked down toward the jetty.

The boat had docked by the time Samuel arrived. Winston, the younger of the two-man crew, was tying it off. He wore the red polyester strip of a soccer team he supported, and bore tattoos on each of his biceps, displaying the names and birth dates of his four children. He'd been working on the supply boat since John's retirement two years before. Still, Chimelu considered him to be inept, a novice, despite being his own son.

Winston smiled at Samuel, nodding his head to music playing in his earphones. Chimelu waved, called, "How's things? Your wall's come down over there, you know." He pointed. "You seen it? Looks like it'll keep you busy for a few days."

"It must have happened in the night," Samuel said.

"You should've used cement. I've been telling you for years, you need cement. I might still have half a bag left over from when we did the extension last year. I'll have a look and bring it for you next time. Just so you can give it a try, see if you prefer it."

Winston had gone below deck to begin unloading the supplies. They could hear him singing, words fumbled, off-key.

"Listen to that nonsense. The boy thinks he's going to be a pop star. There's some or other competition on in the city, and he thinks he's going to win." He shook his head. "Since when did it become too shameful to have a good honest job, I want to know," he shouted down below. "We can't all be famous and rich! Some of us have to do the fucking work!"

Samuel turned away from the shouting, looked out at the water, the pink streaks of clouds, and a sun slow to rise.

"That is another thing," said Chimelu, following Samuel's gaze, "the weather. It looks normal to me for this time of year, doesn't it?"

"Yes, I would say so."

"Well, Keb, down at the harbor, he says the fish aren't running the way they should. He says the tides are unreliable. Or was it unpredictable? I can't remember. But what he did say, and I remember this very clearly, he said he caught a shark in his nets, half-starved, he said, probably hadn't eaten in ages, he said. When has that ever happened before? I can't tell you. I don't think it ever has. Times are bad. They say this is the worst fishing season in living memory."

"They say that every year, Dad," said Winston, coming up from below deck with a box on his shoulder. "They said it when I was a boy and they're still saying it."

"Did anyone ask your opinion? Why aren't you off-loading? Get that stuff down and stop your jabbering." He rolled his eyes at Samuel. "These young ones. No respect. And you have to watch them all day long. But he's a good boy really, in his way. Give me ten years to show him the ropes and he might turn out all right." He climbed down onto the jetty and went to shake Samuel's hand. "Are you well? You look tired."

"No, I'm well. And yourself?"

Chimelu took off his hat and scrunched it into his back pocket. "What can I complain about? Nothing. We're all in good health, thanks be to God. Eshe—that's Winston's second oldest, remember, you saw a photo of her that time—she's in a play at the nursery school this Saturday. One line to say, that's it. One line and Edith has been sewing her costume for two weeks, day and night. A million sequins and ribbons and little shiny things. And when she's not sewing, she's out selling tickets to all the ladies from the church to come and watch. Eshe walks around all day using a hairbrush as a microphone, practicing her line. I can't understand a fucking word she says. But it's pretty cute anyway, even if I'm the one that says so. Winston! Where's the boxes?"

"Right in front of you, Dad. I'm just bringing the last few."

Chimelu pointed at the boxes as though he had put

them there himself. "So, Sam, it's the same stuff as always, but I got a new brand of washing powder. Edith swears by it and it was on special offer. If you don't like it, then just tell me, okay? And we got that manure you asked for. Fucking hell, it stank up the place, I can tell you. I'm glad to be rid of it."

He picked up one of the cardboard boxes and said, "This is from Edith, things from the shop, you know. No, no, I'll carry it. Don't worry. Winston! Is that everything?"

"Yes, Dad."

"So then run up to the cottage and get the water boiled and the tea made. You can bring up all of this when you're done."

Samuel wanted to step out in front of Winston, say, "No, you can't come today. Go away, for God's sake, leave me alone." But he clenched his jaw, put his hand into his pocket, where the lighthouse key warmed in his closed fist. He walked slowly beside Chimelu, his legs suffering as he moved.

Chimelu said, "Did you hear about the mess in parliament? No, I suppose you couldn't, could you? Well, it's chaos, I tell you. Absolute chaos. Corruption scandals everywhere, fraud, opposition parties protesting in the house. This is just in the last fortnight, you know. In the end they had to send in the military and it was a fucking mess. A real fucking mess. I mean, someone like you, Sam, that must kill you to hear that. All those years you spent in jail for standing up to the Dictator and now here we are again calling on the military. And, I'm sorry to say this to you, but to be honest, a lot of people there, on the mainland, a lot of people miss those days. Yes, we were frightened, I mean that goes without saying. But the thing is that at least there was order, there wasn't all this crime. Now it's just a mess."

He paused a moment as they reached the headland, and held a hand to his chest. "It gets me every time, this hill. I can feel my heart beating in my fucking ears. I don't know how you do it, Sam, I really don't." After a few moments he gestured loosely with his arm, showing that he was ready to continue. He breathed out heavily, cleared his throat, began talking again, "Like I said, it's a mess over there, on the mainland. Don't get me started on the roads. Like one giant pothole. Remember how good they were? Well, they had to be, right, what with all those military processions and convoys of Rolls-Royces, huh? This president just flies everywhere. What does he care if the roads are shit?"

By now they had reached the cottage, and Samuel pushed past Chimelu to enter before him. He grabbed the blanket from the couch and threw it across one of the armrests, while Chimelu went to the kitchen and put the box on the table. Samuel waited for him to notice the pot and plate, the fork and spoon, and two mugs on the drying rack. Waited for him to say, "Been having a party?" but Winston had already taken the mugs, and if Chimelu noticed the rest, it made no impression on him. He went back to the living room, sat on the couch with a sigh. "You know what you need, Sam? A footstool. Nothing like a footstool to rest your feet on."

"Maybe I can make one. I have some wood."

"That's all you need. Some wood and a cushion. Winston! Look in that box I put there. Your mother sent biscuits. Not homemade, I'm afraid, Sam. She's been up to her eyeballs in sequins all week, sewing that fucking costume."

Winston came in carrying three mugs, keeping the plastic orange one for himself. He passed the packet of biscuits around. Chimelu took a bite, grimaced, and then read the label. " 'Tropical punch flavor. The taste of Hawaii.' Fucking hell, who invents this shit?" But he took another, holding it in his hand as he finished the first. "It's nice out here," he said, leaning back. "You have it all. Good thing, too, you know, being so far from the mainland. There's talk of a revolution, maybe another coup."

Samuel swallowed the crumbs in his mouth with a sip of tea. It was too sweet. Winston always made the tea too sweet. "They've been speaking about revolution for a long time. Nothing ever happens."

"I know, but the word is that this time it's for real. There's been graffiti and I heard there are underground meetings. It's like the '60s again. Though you'd know more about that than I would."

"Well, I suppose we can only wait and see if it happens."

"Yes, not much else we can do, us old men." He took

another biscuit. "Oh, wait, before I forget, there's been another refugee boat that sunk. You know, one of those illegal ones. Just a few kilometers from here, off our coast. When was it, two days ago?"

"Three," said Winston.

"Three. Three days. There were bodies floating everywhere they say, and so I said to Keb, 'those sharks of yours won't be starving anymore!' He laughed at that, I tell you. Laughed until he spat. Here, Winston, show Sam. You have it saved on your phone, don't you? It's been all over the news, you know. There's nothing else. Just this boat sinking."

Winston brought the phone out of his pocket and sat on the blanketed armrest beside Samuel. "Hold it like this," he said, placing Samuel's hands on either side of the phone. "Now press that triangle in the middle. Yes, that one. Yes, on the screen. Press it."

In his hands there was the image of people, piled high and tight on a boat made invisible by their number. Not even as it began to break up underneath them could it be seen. There were only bodies. Bodies tumbling, falling, slapping the water with open hands. The screen was small in Samuel's grip. It could not contain all the bodies. He shifted his fingers, as though making room for the people. The video stopped.

"What did I do?" he asked.

"Don't worry, we can unpause it. Just keep your fingers like this, okay? There you go," said Winston.

Again they were in the water, sinking, scattering. It

was strangely quiet, despite the panic that he could see. Across the distance there was calling, wailing, but only faintly. Already people were drowning on the little screen. A blur of hair, light brown and long, blew into view, blew away again. The person filming made no sound. Not a gasp or cry.

The video stopped and Samuel stared for a moment, waiting to see if there was more.

"That's it. That's the end," Winston said.

"Can I see it again?"

"Sure, there you go. I'll just go bring up the last few things from the boat."

Once more he watched it. This time he brought the screen up close, looking into it for the face of the man in the tower. But the screen was too small, the people too many. If the man had been on the boat, Samuel could not see him.

"They deserve it, don't they?" said Chimelu. "Anyone stupid enough to pack themselves in a rotting boat like that and try to enter another country illegally is asking to die."

Samuel gave him the phone. "Why did you show me this? No one cared about the refugees before."

"No, but it's some kind of international incident now. The government wants all the bodies. I've heard there are rewards, but I don't think that's true. Anyway, they're looking, that's the main point. Did you find any?"

"Bodies? No, I didn't find a body."

"Well, don't be surprised if a few wash up. Keep your eyes open. There were hundreds on that boat, you saw it yourself."

Winston knocked on the open cottage door. "I left the manure out by the garden, Uncle Sam, is that okay?"

"Yes, thank you."

"Well," said Chimelu, "I suppose it's time for us to go. Take care of yourself, Sam. You're looking tired. Why don't you take the day off? Fix the wall another time, huh? Wait until I bring that cement for you."

"Maybe."

"Good man. No, no, don't come all the way down with us. We know the way. You stay here and rest a bit. See you next time. Take care, okay?"

As they walked away down the slope, Samuel could hear the drone of Chimelu's voice: "Yes, my son, old Sam's not long for this world now. Did you see how he was today? I tell you, it pains me to say it, but we have to accept it. This could be the last time we see poor old Sam alive."

The key would not budge. He could not get it to turn at all. He had to go back to the cottage and fetch an oil can from the hallway. He dribbled some onto the key. When he tried again, his fingers slid on the oily surface, coming away smeared orange with rust. He took a rag from his pocket and clasped the key with it, forcing it to turn. The metal grated, rust flaked from the lock. He shouldered the door open, then wiped his hands on the seat of his trousers; a piece of skin had been loosened on his forefinger and it dragged a little on his pocket. He brought the finger to his mouth, pulled the skin off, felt it on his tongue before spitting it out.

"You can come down now," he called up the stairwell. "They're gone."

He listened but there was no reply, only the sound of the wind through a broken windowpane. He called again. "Come down. It's safe." Then, when the man still did not appear, Samuel climbed the stairs to the top of the tower.

The light filled most of the circular room. There was nowhere to hide, and the man stood, crouching a little, behind the glass prisms. They distorted his form, refracting parts of his arm, a cheek, a patch of shirt many times over. Until Samuel rounded the light, came face-to-face with him, he had seemed jagged, something splintered and put back together poorly.

"They're gone," he said, but still the man hunched behind the glasses. Samuel walked over to one of the windowpanes that enclosed the room. He beckoned to the man, and pointed out the boat making its way back to the mainland. "See, they're gone."

The man frowned, put out his hand to touch the window but, feeling himself watched, pulled it back, put it in his pocket. He cleared his throat, pressed a toe into a crack in the concrete floor, moved across the room to another windowpane, and looked out. Then he circled the room, his feet *slap-slapping* as he surveyed the view through each of the panes until he reached Samuel again. The supply boat was gone from view now, had probably already docked at the other side.

The man pointed at Samuel, then at the mainland, made a circle with his finger that seemed to be indicating the island. He spoke a few words; a question by their tone.

Samuel thought for a moment, said, "It depends what you're asking. I used to live there, yes. But if you want to know if I go back, if I'll ever go back, then the answer is no."

He did not elaborate, did not say that once he had very nearly made the journey. It had been a long time ago, three or four years after his employment as lighthouse keeper had begun. Back then the supply boat had come once a week, more often if he radioed. With each visit, John and Chimelu had worked at him, insisting that things had changed under the new regime, that the president was a good man, that life was different, better.

"You don't have to be afraid," said John. "Half the military are in jail now. The rest are at the bases. It's not like it was. We're free people again."

Chimelu, who was still young then, said, "Come on, Sam. You can't be alone all the time like this. When was the last time you were with a woman?"

"Shut up," said John.

But Chimelu insisted, "What? It's not healthy. You can get all stopped up and get cancer or something."

"Don't listen to him, Sam. He's an idiot. Just come across for a couple of hours. Have a walk in the market, drink a beer. Relax a bit and enjoy it. I promise I'll have you back before sunset."

Samuel could no longer remember why he had, in the end, agreed to go. He only remembered being on the boat, that Chimelu threw a moldy life vest at him, and then, seeing him struggle with it, showed him how to put it on. Around his neck he had a small leather pouch in which he kept his money. He had not worn it in a long time, and he was sensitive to its presence, to the weight of coins pressing into the fold beneath his ribs. The cord chafed his neck, its knot rough with damp in the morning fog. He repositioned himself, rolled his shoulders, fiddled with the collar of the life vest so that he might feel less constricted.

When the engine started and the boat moved backward, away from the jetty, Samuel reeled a little, feeling that he was about to sprawl across the deck. But he caught himself, gripped the crate that was his seat, then sat back, the vest now up around his chin, over his ears and high at the back of his neck. He waited for seasickness, and several times thought it had arrived—a stomach rumble, extra saliva in his mouth. But the symptoms didn't develop further.

He clasped his hands together and looked out at the nearby sea and sky, gray echoes of one another in the mist. By now the boat had turned a wide arc, and was facing the mainland, chugging white froth behind them. The land was no more than a shadow, something long and flat and distant, with a single light that wavered ahead of them.

John called Chimelu to take over in the wheelhouse and came to sit beside Samuel. He pointed into the mist, showing two shapes that he said were fishing boats. "There'll be more of them out there that we can't see now. There's good fishing in this bay. When I was a boy my mother would send us to the harbor and we'd strip down, dive into the water, and grab fish with our hands.

No rods or nets, nothing like that. Just our bare hands. You ever try it like that?"

"No. I've never fished."

"Never?"

"No. I can't swim."

"Well, that's no reason. You get a rod and just do it off the rocks there on your island. You don't need to swim for that."

"Maybe."

"There's no maybe about it. Fresh fish—there's nothing better in the world. It's delicious. I get hungry just thinking about it." He paused. "Anyway, it'll give you a way to pass the time, some fishing, you know. You have to be bored out there, all alone with nothing to do all day, no one to talk to."

"I'm okay. I don't mind it."

Still, he had wondered what it might be like to be among people again. Footfalls in the streets, morning greetings, market haggling, the jostle of bars, laughter in the cinema. In the park, conversations overheard. Children playing. Women stopping to chatter. Cigarette smoke and street food. The noise of pigeons, of dogs barking. Each of these came to life where he sat on the boat. People and noises pressing in around him. A great crowd forming in order to crush him.

The life vest was too tight. He pulled at it, but it remained firm at the back of his neck, high on his chin. The smell of it was strong: something never cleaned, something aging toward decay. He turned his face upward, but the smell pursued him. Rot in his nose, mold on his skin. Against his midsection the money pouch had turned into a lump of ice. It burned there, the cold feeling its way inward until his organs were frozen hard. He gasped, sucked the air, looked to John with eyes white with panic.

But John had moved away, and was standing at the prow, a hand shielding his eyes—for the mist had lifted suddenly, vanished as though it had never been there, and the sun was a brightness in the water ahead of them.

The harbor was visible now. People moved on the concrete length of it, each movement clear. Voices, too, reached them, sounds Samuel had only just been imagining, and the panic was hard within him, freezing a cough so that it turned into a splutter.

A boat, recently returned, was being unloaded. Men upended crate after crate of fish onto the dock. Bodies slid and twitched, a mass of them, gasping where they lay and overlay one another. Hands reached into that mass, taking knives to their guts, even as they writhed. Around them the pooling water became pink with innards.

The crowd pressed in tighter around Samuel. There was breath on his face, there were voices, hands reaching out to him. Samuel spoke through the apparitions, "Take me back." Then louder, as he had not been heard. "Take me back!"

John turned, removed his hand from his brow. "What are you saying, Sam? We're here now. We can't go back yet."

Samuel scrabbled up, clasped the side of the wheelhouse, turning away from the mainland. He could hardly breathe. "No. Take me back. I want to go home."

They walked down the stairs, Samuel's shoulder following the curve of the staircase. He was unsteady in his movements, as though, despite the years in between, he had never left that boat; as though he were still aboard, crying out that he wanted to return to his home. The stairs, each of them a wave, rose to meet him, threatening to knock him over.

The man followed him closely. His breath was on Samuel's neck, causing him to hasten forward. He wanted to reach the cottage, lock the door, bar the windows, keep the man out, and by that action make him disappear from the island. For the man had spoken to him up there in the tower: had spoken, pointing at himself, saying the garble of his name before pressing against the window and gesturing down at the roof of the cottage. Then he had turned to look at Samuel.

Samuel had made as though he did not understand. He moved across the room, whistling something tuneless. The man tried to follow him, but Samuel kept himself in motion, the lens always between them. He knew what the man had been saying and he did not want to hear it again: "I am to live here now." Samuel had not thought of that, had not considered what would become of the man after the boat had left. But he was here, with no place to go other than where he had come from, nor any means of getting there. He was here. He was here to stay.

Samuel went to the top of the stairwell, looked back over his shoulder, and saw the man refracted a hundred times over. Behind the man was the sea, and him upon it, hundreds of him, floating on the water, searching for a place to land.

Now, in his descent, the man pursuing him, Samuel moved as swiftly as he could toward the certainty of the cottage. If only the stairs, rolling on and on, breaking against his shuffling feet, would pause for a moment. Only a moment, so that his head could stop reeling, the gathering saliva settle. In that pause he would cross the intervening space without strain.

Coming out of the darkness of the tower, Samuel faltered, blind for an instant as the light caught at him. Then something caused him to lose his balance and topple forward down the three outside steps, landing hard in the sand below. At first he did not move. He was winded and his breath came loudly. His palms stung. His left knee was in pain. And somewhere, maybe his chin, there was blood that he could smell.

He had been tripped. The man had made him fall,

that was what had happened. The man was keeping him from returning home. Samuel raised his head a little. The cottage was twenty yards away, its door open. All around him came the sound of water. He became dizzied, lowered his head. The waves caught him in their ebb and flow, carrying him nowhere.

"I want to go home," he said. "Take me home."

A hand was on him, lifting him from the ground. Sun blinded, he could see nothing, only hear a voice saying, "Are you all right? Do you need some help?"

"I knew it," Samuel said. "I knew you could speak."

The man's face cleared into view, dark and expressionless. His mouth was not moving, though he continued to speak. "Let me help you. Where are you going?"

"Home."

The man helped him inside the cottage, put him to lie on the couch. Around Samuel everything was shadows and darkness. The sea was gone now, the waves. There were other sounds. Traffic, people. The rumble of trucks and cars, motorbikes, buses. People calling. The barking of a dog. Beneath him the couch gave way to hardness, to sunbaked concrete. Above him a woman was asking, "Are you all right, Uncle?"

Her feet were white in places, white with cracking and dryness. Yet when he looked up, her round face was damp, her fat rolls marked out on her dress by patches of sweat. She struggled to bend down over her belly, and panted a little as she said, "Come, Uncle, you can't lie here in the dirt." She helped him up with wet hands. His fingers slipped and he thought he might fall, crack his skull on the wall behind him.

"Where are you going?"

Samuel pointed at the wall.

The woman wiped the sweat from her face and spoke slowly. "No, Uncle. That's the Palace, the prison, you see. You've just come from there. I was across the road. I saw them release you."

"Yes, I live there."

"No, Uncle, you can't live there anymore. You're free now. You can't go back. Don't you have a family? Where was your home? Can you go there?"

"I don't know."

The woman put her damp arm around him, led him across the street to sit on a cinder block under a tarpaulin spread for shade. Beside the block was a pile of empty sweet wrappers—yellow, bright pink, and blue—and kebab sticks stained in places where there had been meat. The woman handed Samuel a plastic bottle, murky with fingerprints, and he drank the lukewarm water, while she wafted a dirty rag at a row of cooked sheep's heads laid out on greasy newspaper. Behind her a washing line hung, black with cuts of meat, pairs of chicken feet, and calves' tongues. Flies rose lazily as she waved the rag, then returned, were waved away again, and finally allowed to settle down to feed.

"How long were you in there, Uncle?" the woman asked.

"I can't remember. Maybe it was twenty-five years, I don't know."

"It's no wonder you're confused."

"I'm not confused. It's my home."

"A prison can't be your home." She passed him a skewer of dark meat. "Eat this."

He took it and chewed with difficulty, his remaining teeth loose in his mouth. He hunched in on himself as he sucked at the meat, moving away from the onslaught of buildings and people, the roar of traffic and motion. None of it had been there before he'd gone inside. It had all been quiet then, mostly grazing land. Sometimes, between the picks and sledgehammers he might have caught the lowing of cattle, a herd boy's whistle or song. It was gone now. Only this in its stead. This chaos, bordered by grinning sheep's heads as he chewed and chewed and chewed, waiting to remember to swallow.

After their time in the labor yard that first day, they were taken single file through three different corridors lined with cells. At the end of the last one, a guard unlocked a door that had recently been painted. Even so, the bars were already grimed with fingerprints, and the naked cement walls bore similar marks, prints that continued up the height of them and across the ceiling. Had prisoners played a game, seeing who could leap highest, leave a handprint? Perhaps they had stood on one another's shoulders, trying to tilt the roof to let in a little air, for there was no window and the brown-crusted bucket in the middle of the room was heavy with flies and stink. In places the cement floor was dark with urine that had not yet dried.

Beside the open door was a pile of grass mats. Each prisoner took one as he entered the cell, then found a place to be seated. Once all the mats had been claimed and the room was full, the guard said, "Move up, move along. There's plenty more to come." Nine men were waiting to enter, watching as those inside shuffled together, making space as they were able. One of the nine, a man with a side parting shaved into his hair, came and sat beside Samuel. He crossed his legs, smiled, waited for the guard to lock the door and leave, before turning to Samuel and saying, "I wonder if they'll feed us." There was no overhead light in the cell, but the lights in the corridor were strong and shone in, keeping the cell bright. Samuel could see grains of sand from the yard in the curl of the man's ear, and more sitting between his scalp and hair. He had two healing bruises on his face and a ring of scabs around each wrist. He was fiddling with the left ring, pulling at it until a piece came loose. He inspected it, then put it in his mouth. He saw Samuel watching him and smiled. "Don't worry. I'm not a cannibal." He laughed a little, a chuckle at the back of his throat. "They say the Dictator is one, that he eats all his enemies. Have you heard that? He ate the president, ate him raw."

"That's not true," said Samuel. "The president was shot and thrown into a ditch. They found his body. It was all still there. No one ate it."

"Oh," said the man. He looked disappointed. "Well, I suppose if he ate all his enemies he'd be much fatter than he already is. I didn't think it was true actually. I was just saying. You know, because you hear things."

Around them the other prisoners were settling down

for the night, trying to get comfortable. The man moved closer to Samuel to make way for another's legs. "I'm Roland," he said.

"Samuel."

"Were you in the march at the square?"

"Yes."

"Me too. I went with some people from the college. I'm studying to be a teacher, science and maths mostly, but we have to do English as well. We have our exams in two weeks' time."

Samuel nodded, watching as Roland lay down, his legs curled up in the space left for him. Roland began to murmur to himself, from time to time shaking his head and starting over again with whatever it was that he was reciting. Samuel leaned his back against the wall, lifted his head, counted the handprints that were scattered above him. Somewhere, in one of the many corridors, a man was screaming.

The next day, and for most of the days to follow, there was food. Never much, but enough to let them sleep and rise and work. Six days a week they broke rocks in the yard, and though the hammers were never altered unless damaged, some days they seemed lighter, others heavier. Sunday mornings they were woken by the static of a preacher's sermon, fed to them through a horned loudspeaker mounted in the corridor. For an hour the air bristled with the news that the Dictator had been chosen by God and, like God, he was their benevolent father. He loved them. He wanted great things for them. Great things that he himself would bestow on them. All he asked for in return was obedience. Was that too much to expect? Obedience in the face of so much love?

Some of the prisoners muttered or frowned, causing the guard to tap his rifle against the bars, to hiss, "Shut up and listen!"

Samuel examined his broken fingernails, looked around the cell at the expressions of the other men, watched Roland close his eyes as he mouthed words to himself. The day brought nothing else after the sermon. There was no relief from the cramped, airless cell, nothing to do but watch one another shit and doze.

A fortnight came and went slowly. Roland said, "Well, it looks like I'll have to take the exams next semester. I just need to make sure I don't forget things while I'm in here." He began to recite with increasing fervor, and each night said to Samuel, "It'll probably be tomorrow. I think it will be. They won't keep us for more than a month, not more than a month surely."

Soon men started being removed from the yard, or were fetched from the cell in the night. Roland said, "You see, Samuel, you see." But when those same men returned hours or days later, black with torture and beatings, he did not say anything, only looked at them darkly. One night he shook Samuel awake. "These men are idiots," he said. "It must be that they're being asked to swear allegiance to the Dictator and are refusing. Don't you think? That's why they're being beaten. Listen, Samuel, when they come for us we must do it, we must swear. We say yes, and we go back to life, and I take my exams and become a teacher. It isn't wrong. It isn't wrong to do that. He's not so bad after all, not really. So, we're agreed, we swear, okay? We swear."

Samuel patted him on the shoulder. "We swear," though he knew it would not be as simple as that.

The next week they came for Roland while he was working in the yard. He smiled, showed Samuel a thumbs-up. He did not return.

Samuel woke on the couch. The man was kneeling beside him, saying his name. He was holding out a cup of tea. Steam was coming off it, a few sugar grains glistened on the inside lip. The man had gone into the kitchen, been in the cupboards. Samuel pushed the cup away, watching as the tea slopped onto the carpet. He sat up with difficulty and brought his hands to his face to rub his eyes; he saw the fresh grazes on his palms and remembered his fall. He moved aside, just a little, away from where the man knelt, before putting his fingertips to his eyes. He felt that he had been dreaming, but couldn't recall what the dream had contained—he had been somewhere, or had been about to say or do something perhaps, something waiting to be completed, to be remembered. He shook his head, pressed harder at his eyes until his palms were against his cheeks and he felt the sting of the grazes, and on his chin, a wound hardening.

It was the prison blisters he remembered now, and it

was like stepping back into the dream he'd been having, stepping back into it but finding it changed, and needing to locate himself in it. Here were the blisters on his hands, blisters that filled and emptied, and never seemed to heal. They were worst with water, those days when the prisoners were allowed to wash, the wounds burning, softening. Afterward his hands cracked and flaked, and he picked at the skin nervously. He did this each time he was taken to the interrogation room, no matter how many times he'd been called there before, no matter the years.

He was afraid in that room, though he had never been threatened beyond the first time. Still, he feared it—the intimidation of death, of violence—and it made him sick. Made him mumble and fabricate and chew his own skin. He wondered when they would have done with him, when he might be set free. And once, after he'd got to know his interrogators well enough, he asked them about Roland, about why he had been offered the opportunity to swear loyalty, and why that choice had not been given to Samuel.

"What are you talking about?" said Bila. He was the older of the two officials, rougher. He did not always shave, came in some days with gray stubble and the smell of beer on him.

"The student teacher," said Samuel. "We came in together. He was freed last year."

"That's what you think? You think he's out there, outside, teaching. Someone like that? You think that's how it works? You swear to follow the Dictator and you're allowed out?"

"Isn't that what happened? Where is he then?"

"You don't have to know that. Your job is to tell us what we want to know."

"Are you saying he's dead? Is that it? He was harmless. He didn't know anything."

The other man, Essien, who suffered from a skin condition that had stained parts of his body white, took out a cigarette, lit it, and passed it to Samuel.

"Come on," he said, "let's go. What do you have for us this week? What do you know?"

And, as he had done each other time, Samuel gave names, reported what was said in the cell, answered queries about activities happening outside, about organizations and movements and people he had never heard of. In exchange, he was not beaten, was given a cup of sweet coffee and a sandwich, was allowed to live.

Of course, the other prisoners suspected him. They wondered at his continued interrogations, from which he returned always unharmed. In time they began to shy away from him, to greet him with coldness and stares. They slept with their backs to him, spoke in whispers when he was near. He waited to be smothered in his sleep or stabbed with something made sharp out of sight of the guards. In the yard he expected murder at all times, the blow of a hammer, sudden, too quick for him to scream. Death was at his shoulder, waiting.

But he was never touched. The prisoners believed

him to be a person of value to the officials, believed that if he were harmed, they would be punished, would be taken from the cell and not seen again. So he was left alone. New prisoners, when they came, were told to keep away from him, were told a man like that, a man of cowardice, was contagious, was in permanent quarantine.

Samuel rose from the couch, moved across the room toward the kitchen. He was still a little unsteady, and clasped the back of the couch, the doorway, and the kitchen's ladderback chair. The man followed, held his arms out behind Samuel, waiting for him to fall.

"I'm not dead yet," he said, and then, when the man looked at him in query, shouted, "I'm not dead! Not yet, damn you!"

The man stepped away, his hands raised.

Samuel leaned against the sink, opened the tap, and washed his hands, soaping the grit out of his wounds. Then he splashed water on his face, watching it turn to pink as it dripped back into the basin. He could not shake his dreaming. He was still in the prison, within its walls. Yet despite the time he had spent there, he was left with no more than a scattering of memories. As though it had not been years at all, but only a day. One day that he had lived over and over, and was still living now.

He dried his face, wiped his hands, and crossed the

room again. He ought to go outside, to clear his mind. But he felt that he was trapped inside the cottage, that he could not leave. At the kitchen doorway, he looked back. He had heard a whisper. At the table, beside the man, they were sitting, the two interrogators. Bila was saying, "Wait a moment before you go. I forgot to tell you. Your father is dead."

Samuel said nothing. He put his hand down, found a door, a doorknob. In the corridor a guard was standing, waiting to escort him back to the yard. This was in the ninth year, or perhaps the tenth, when the uniforms had changed from khaki to black. The guard's boots were dull, and on his trousers, below each knee, were patches of dust that hadn't been rubbed off well enough after kneeling. Had the man been praying?

"He was part of the Independence Movement, wasn't he?" said Bila.

"Yes."

Bila was finishing a cigarette. Essien had a mug in his hand, but was not drinking.

"He was shot, if I'm right, during a protest," said Bila.

"It crippled him."

"It must have been very hard for him, a man like that, to have a son like you. A rebel, against independence, against the country."

"I was never against the country, never against independence. It was the shit that came after that I was against."

Bila threw his cigarette butt on the floor. There were others there already, twenty of them at least, a few still smoldering, marking the floor in rounds of black.

"Say what you want, the truth is you've cost your father the decency of a burial."

"What do you mean?"

Essien put down his mug, licked his lips. "It's a law now. You have to get a certificate of permission to bury your dead."

"A certificate?" said Samuel. "I don't understand. What's the problem?"

"Certificates of permission are denied those affiliated with or related to rebels."

Samuel put his hand to his forehead, pinched an eyebrow. "So, what will happen to him?"

Bila shrugged, but Essien said, "I don't know. Some people, I've heard that some people are burying their loved ones in their gardens."

"We have no garden."

Bila stood up. "Listen, man, it's not our problem. We passed on the news. That's it. That's all." He walked from the room, ignoring the guard's salute.

Essien stood, too, walked to where Samuel waited. He put a hand on his shoulder. "He was in the Movement. Someone will help. Someone will give him a space in their yard. He won't be left, I'm sure."

"It doesn't make any sense. This law. It doesn't make any sense."

Essien looked out into the corridor, put his head

close to Samuel's ear. "Things are bad outside. No one is safe. The Dictator is paranoid. He fears everyone. I've taught my children to sleep with their hands over their mouths. Who knows what they might say in their sleep and who could be listening?"

After that time Samuel was called only once more to the interrogation room. Bila had retired by then, and the new man, who carried a folder of documents and wore a suit and tie, was senior to Essien. He did not believe in cigarettes and sweetened coffee. He asked Samuel several questions, mentioned organizations and people, referred to other prisoners. Samuel fumbled answers, but the man was not fooled. He said, "This prisoner knows nothing. He's wasting our time. There are real enemies to freedom that we need to catch. Put him back to work. We have no use for him anymore."

In the years that followed, years of being ignored by his fellow prisoners, weeks could pass without the need for Samuel to talk at all. He lived in silence, at night forced to take up a place in the corner, pressed against the bars of the cell. He thought back on conversations he had had in his past, of his interrogations even, to fill the loneliness. He longed to turn to his neighbor, to whisper a few words, to have someone answer him.

Guards were ever changing at the Palace. They were moved across the country to different institutions and situations, so that no man could build strong ties with others. One year, for several months, the corridor had a fat, middle-aged guard. He was kind, didn't shout or kick them. "Do unto others," he would say, and at night he wished them all a pleasant sleep as he walked the corridor, singing hymns to himself. He was named Disciple, and explained when asked, "It's not the name my parents gave me, but it is the one God gave me when I came to him, first as a sinner, then as a follower."

One night he stopped where Samuel sat, his head against the bars, arms around his knees. "I've been watching you, brother. You're not well. You don't sleep. Your soul is in torment."

Samuel didn't look up. "What do you know about any of it?"

"Just what I can see. It's in your face. You must release the demons living inside you. God will forgive you your sins, as he forgave me mine. He is ready and waiting. You only have to ask."

"You're wrong. I have asked. He sent me away."

"Now that can't be true, brother."

"Can't it?" said Samuel, looking up, frowning. "Look at me, I've betrayed every person I know, and many that I don't. I'm surrounded by men who would like nothing more than to see me dead."

"Yes, you have betrayed some, that is true, but the important thing is that you have shown loyalty to the one that matters, His Supreme Highness, Protector of the Nation and Savior of the People."

"You mean to God? I've never been loyal to him."

"No, not God. I mean our great ruler, the Dictator as some know him. This is his official title."

"That is his title? All of that?"

"I believe there is some more, but I can't remember it all."

"I suppose I shouldn't be surprised that he's given himself a name like that. Do you remember the victory parade, after the coup? All that expense and show?"

"Of course I remember it," Disciple said. He smiled, tapped a finger lightly on one of the cell bars. "I was there. He freed us, brought us salvation from a president who had betrayed us all. A president who had put his cronies in positions of power and who then went on to take everything for themselves. All the rest, the people, and everything else, it was all forgotten."

"How is that different from the Dictator and his motorcade full of his brothers and friends and cousins? He placed them in positions of power too. How is that different? And all the people he murdered?"

"No, brother, come, that is enough. He has saved us. After all your years in prison, do you still not know that?"

Samuel was silent for a moment. He turned his head a little, looked back at the men sleeping around him. "Do you want to know what I know after all these years?"

"Tell me."

"I know that I have no idea what my child looks like. In my mind he's still a baby, he's still a tiny little baby that I last saw in the arms of my mother on the morning that I went to the march on the square. For me, nothing has changed outside, everything has stood still around that baby. My sister is a teenager, my baby's mother is still marching on the statue, my parents are both alive. Nothing has changed. Even in here I forget that time has passed. Sometimes I catch my reflection in a window. I don't recognize myself. Who is that man, I want to say."

"You don't have to ask that question. As I've said, he's a man who has shown himself to be loyal."

Samuel turned to look at the guard again. "Don't say that. I've never been loyal to anyone but myself."

Late afternoon, the threat of rain was gray overhead. Samuel dissolved yeast in a metal bowl filled with warm water. He added sugar and salt, and let it stand awhile as he retrieved the old biscuit tin in which he kept the flour. He made no measurements, judging how much to pour by experience.

The man sat at the table across from him, watching. He leaned back in the chair, his legs wide, and dug his fingers into the packet of tropical punch biscuits. The plastic packaging rustled as he fumbled for one, and then still more as he pulled it out. He put the entire thing in his mouth and chewed loudly, his lips partly open. Samuel went to put his hands in the bowl, caught the man's eye as he observed his movements. He groped for another biscuit, put it in his mouth, still chewing the other.

Samuel looked down. There was dirt in the ridges of his knuckles and under his nails, and some still clung to his grazed palms. He went to the basin and used dishwashing liquid to clean his hands again, drying them on an old brown towel that hung at the front of the oven. Then he returned to the table and began to mix the dough. It balled under his pressure, became elastic, warm. He placed the bowl on the counter and draped the towel over it, giving the dough time to rise.

When he turned around again, the man was using a fingertip to draw in flour that had spilled on the table. It was an idle act, no more than a doodle. Yet as Samuel approached, the man hastily erased it, brushing the flour off the table and into his waiting hand. He held it out to Samuel, a question.

"Over there," Samuel said, pointing to a gray plastic bin. He packed away the ingredients, wiped down the table with a dry rag, letting the remaining flour fall to the floor. He lifted the box sent by Edith onto the table, smoothing back the folds of the lid to prevent them from bouncing back. The man had resumed eating the biscuits. He put a finger in his mouth, hooked it into a tooth, loosened something, and then licked it from his nail before carrying on chewing. Samuel looked down into the box and lifted out a pile of tatty-edged, cheap-papered magazines. The top one bore a cover image of a woman in a silver dress, her eyelids thick with fake lashes. Beside her stood a man, shirtless but for a collar and a silver bow tie. He had pierced nipples, tattooed arms. Samuel recognized the photo. He already had a copy of that magazine. He went through the pile, picking out the duplicates, tossing them into a wooden crate in which he kept paper for starting fires.

Next were the video cassettes. Their cases were tacky to the touch, smelled of cigarettes and closed boxes. On one of them someone had spilled tomato sauce and had allowed it to dry to a crust. There were nine videos in total, none that he had yet seen.

The man reached across the table and picked up the videos, examining them as a customer might do in a shop. He ate the last biscuit, upended the packet over his mouth so that he could catch the crumbs. He walked to the bin, threw the packet away, burped softly. Then, smelling of crumbs and artificial fruit, he came to where Samuel stood, put his hand in the box, brought out three glass jam jars, half a pink-and-gold striped pencil, and a straw still in its paper envelope.

Samuel shook his head at the man and took the straw from him. The box was his. He would unpack it himself. The man shrugged, sat back down, and watched as out came a coffee tin of mismatched buttons, a bag of cable ties and wires, a ceramic bear holding a faded-to-orange heart, a cracked dinner plate with a picture of a pineapple on it. At the bottom of the box was a photo album. It was old, ring bound, the cover showing a cartoon of a boy in bell-bottom dungarees holding a watering can. As Samuel lifted it from the box, photos, loosened with time, fell out. He bent down and gathered them off the floor. On the other side of the table the man went down on his hands and knees to retrieve one from where it had slid under the large gas fridge. He looked at it, blinked, skimmed it across the table.

The photo was of a young man, not much more than a teenager, in a military uniform. His beret was slightly crooked, leaning toward his left eyebrow, his neck was stiff; he was not smiling and his eyes were dull, as though he had held the pose for some time without blinking. It was a formal shot: head and shoulders only, the photo bordered in white.

Samuel looked through the others in his hand. A fat lady in an apron stirring a pot over an open fire. Behind her stood a man, his face bright with laughter. The next was of the front of a house. A ladder was leaning against a half-painted wall. Through a window, very faint, a face looked out. Then five young men draped across a park bench, drinking soda from bottles. Again the boy in his uniform, now in front of the painted house, his face turned to the side as if in conversation with someone that could not be seen. Yet another, this time of him facing the camera, smiling. Two of him with people that Samuel took to be his parents, a dog sniffing a bush in the background of both. These photos showed his full body, revealing a boy in discomfort, his stance awkward, as it had been for many others like him: boys unused to wearing shoes, or who wore sandals at the most. Back then it had been a common sight, in those months before and after the coup. New Shoes Boys they were called in mockery of their limping marches, their stumbles when taking the stairs. They were young men mostly, from poor families, or homeless, vulnerable in one way or another. The military sought them out, promised shelter, food, money. More than one of Samuel's street friends had been seduced. Dog was one of them. He had returned to the old neighborhood one weekend to swagger.

"And this?" Samuel had said.

"This what? This new life, you mean? The one where I'm not sleeping in doorways or stealing just enough to get by? This life where I'm not kicked and beaten by police for standing in the wrong place?"

Samuel looked down at the shiny black boots, the rifle slung over Dog's shoulder like a handbag.

"This," said Dog, "this is power. I'm someone people have to listen to. You should do the same. You can't hide under the seats in the cinema forever, watching cops and robbers. Play it in real life."

"You think shoes turn a dog into a person? You'll be a dog all your life."

"At least I'll be more than you ever will."

But that had been a long time ago, before Meria, before the protests. Before prison. Even so, it was Dog he recognized in many of the soldiers and guards each day of his imprisonment. Young men who had no idea what they were doing. Who stood to attention, rattled their rifles on the bars, barked commands they were told to give. And the truth was, at the time, and maybe even long afterward, Samuel had envied Dog those boots. Envied him his uniform. Who didn't want to be more than they were, who didn't want to rise up out of the dirt and be something?

Samuel put the photos aside. The man leaned across the table, picked them up, and went through them slowly as Samuel opened the album. The cellophane had come loose on most of the pages. It flapped as he turned them, and only a few of the photos stayed in place. There was a birthday cake fashioned around a plastic doll so that it looked like a ball gown of pink and white froth. Beside it a girl in a dress of a similar style, her smile broad under a pair of thick glasses. Next a boy—the same one from the uniformed photos, but young now, a child—posing with a handkerchief and pointed fingers to resemble a bandit. Then the boy and the girl in her party dress standing with their backs to closed curtains, holding hands reluctantly, frowning, the tremble of the girl's lip coming out as a disfiguring blur. And though the memory was not his, Samuel was moved by it, his thoughts shifting to a ride in the car of the woman who'd picked him up outside the prison, who'd fed him and given him clothes. Who had taken him to her own home while she tried to locate his family.

"I'm sorry," she'd said, "I can't get any information about a Meria or a Lesi. There is nothing about them, and I'm afraid your mother passed away some years ago. But I've managed to find your sister. I'll take you there, it isn't very far. I'm sure she'll be glad to see you."

When the car stopped, the woman did not get out. She tapped Samuel on the shoulder, as though waking him. "We're here, Uncle."

The street was a busy one, flanked on both sides by

tall blocks of flats, the pavements piled with trash. The woman pointed to a building ten meters ahead. It was painted peppermint green, its windows dark.

"It's that one. Seventh floor, number two. I'm sorry; I can't go in with you. There's no parking allowed here, see?" She showed Samuel a signpost. "I'll circle the block a few times. If you are not out by, well, let's say quarter to, then I'll take it it's all gone well, okay?"

"Yes. Thank you."

Samuel went through a door made entirely of glass. Tiles of green, flecked with gray and black, lined the floor and walls. He climbed the stairs slowly. By the time he reached the seventh floor, he was afraid. But he knocked loudly, waited. The neighboring flat's front door opened, and a woman in a dressing gown came out into the hallway. She had a baby on her hip, a bottle of beer in her hand; two more children clutched at her legs.

"Who you looking for?"

"Mary Martha."

The woman took a sip of beer. "She's number three."

She stayed where she was, watching as he walked down the hall and knocked at the next door. After a while it was opened by a fat middle-aged woman. She wore a white blouse that spread unevenly over her belly and breasts, and below that she had on a pair of gray trousers, black tennis shoes. On her head was a cheap blond wig—long-haired, fringed. She had been frowning when she opened the door and her expression did not change when she saw who it was.

"I wondered when you'd find your way here. I heard the new government's been releasing prisoners."

"Yes."

"I suppose you want to stay here," she said, stepping aside to let him squeeze past her. "And I suppose you want to be fed. There's the kitchen, that way. You can have some bread. I haven't started supper yet. The children will be home late today."

"Thanks," said Samuel. The kitchen was small. With Mary Martha in it beside him, there was hardly space to move.

"Well, take some bread. I'm not doing it for you."

There was bread on the counter, a sliced store loaf, but no butter or other spread. He took a slice from the packet and chewed it dry.

Mary Martha put a hand down into her bosom and brought out a soft pack of cigarettes and a neon yellow lighter. She lit the cigarette as she spoke out of the corner of her mouth. "You heard Lesi died."

He stopped chewing. "No."

"Well, I tried to get the message to you. It's not my fault."

"How?"

"I told someone and they said they knew someone who—"

"No, how did he die. That's what I mean. We've been hearing gunshots and explosions these past months. Was it an explosion?"

"Oh no, not that. It was long before any of that.

Must be something like sixteen years now. He would have been twenty-four this year?"

"Twenty-five."

"So about sixteen, seventeen years then."

"How did he die?"

"Jesus, Samuel, why do you keep asking that? I don't know. He died. He was alive, he had a fever, and then he was dead."

"You didn't go to a hospital or a doctor?"

"With what money? You were gone. Mommy and Daddy were old. I was pregnant and practically alone."

They stood in silence until Mary Martha gestured at the loaf of bread. "Are you done with that?"

He still had three quarters of a slice in his hand. He nodded.

"Then close the packet, dammit. It'll go stale."

He did, twisting the bag and binding it with a small plastic clip.

"You better get a job," she said. "Even if it's begging. I don't care what you do, but you can't just sit around expecting to be looked after like it was in jail. Remember, I have two children—I didn't ask for a third."

Three months Samuel stayed with them. He had no key of his own, and the children would often lock him out in the evening until their mother returned, claiming they heard no knocking over the sound of music or the television. They kept him from using the bathroom, forcing him to the public restrooms in the park where there was no toilet paper, where the doors would not close, where the smells would overwhelm.

"Why is he here?" the boy said. "He stinks. He eats everything. It's because of him that I couldn't get the new shoes you promised me."

"I haven't said anything before because he's supposed to be family," the girl said, "but he watches me through the keyhole when I'm in the shower or in my bedroom. He touches himself. I don't feel safe with him being here. He's going to rape me."

Her brother agreed. "I've seen him doing it. He's done disgusting things in prison and wants to do them here too. He's dangerous."

Soon Mary Martha came home with a newspaper clipping advertising the job at the lighthouse.

"I'll help you get it," she had said, "but then I never want to hear from you again."

That night, in bed, Samuel found it difficult to settle. The bread he'd made earlier had not risen properly; now it was a lump in his stomach. In the lounge he could hear the couch creaking as the man got up; he heard him walk to the front door, open it, step outside. He did not shut the door behind him. Wind gusted in. It made windows rattle, pictures and curtains tremble.

Samuel tutted. Was it necessary for the man to be going again? Only an hour earlier they had met outside the toilet, bumped into each other, in fact. Samuel had gone first to check on the light: the mechanism was still a little out, but he had been unable to fix it just then, reminding himself that it was to be done the next day. Leaving the tower, he had walked to the outhouse, thinking the man was inside the cottage. There, just outside, the man leaving, his eyes down, they had bumped shoulders, catching each other by surprise. An awkward dance followed, each moving to left, to right, blocking the other as they were trying to clear the way.

The front door closed, footsteps sounded. The man was back. A light went on in the kitchen. It crept around the corner of Samuel's doorway, illuminating a part of his cupboard. He could hear water running; a mug being placed on the counter; cutlery being moved. Samuel coughed. The noise stopped. The light went out and in the dark the cutlery was shuffled again. Then silence.

Samuel closed his eyes, began to relax, and then he froze. There were footsteps entering his room. He sat up a little, looked at the tall shadow. "What is it? What do you want? I'm sleeping."

The man came closer. One of his hands seemed to be in a fist. Was he holding something? He sat down at the foot of the bed. Samuel pulled the covers up to his chest, saying again, "What do you want?"

The man began to talk. He pointed outside. He made gestures that Samuel could not identify in the dark. Certain words he repeated, or came back to like the main characters in a story he was telling. Then he leaned forward, took up his right hand, pointed his index finger, and, as though it were a knife, slid it across his throat.

The Third Day

He woke with a start, certain that the man was above him, his teeth bared, a knife in his hands. But the room was empty when he opened his eyes, empty and cool. No one had entered it for some time.

He dressed as he did on any other morning, though the fearful clarity of the man's finger across his throat was with him still. He had tried to reason with himself, thinking that the gesture must mean something different to the man. Though what, he could not guess.

He walked to the doorway, his hands at his neck, and looked out into the living room to see whether the man was awake. Neither of them had remembered to pull closed the curtains the night before, and the room was lighter than it would normally have been at this time of day. The man lay folded on the couch. His right hand was loosely clenched, as though he had been holding something before allowing it to fall. Samuel watched, and thought how easy it would be to shoot the man. How easy to simply lift his arm and shoot him as he slept. Afterward, he would not bury the man within the island's stone wall. No. This body would be returned to the site where it had beached itself. Samuel would wade out with it as far as he could, let the waves take it, watch them carry it back to where it had come from. There would be a mess, that was certain. He would have to wipe down the walls, probably burn the couch. He would make an excuse for its loss, beg Chimelu to ask Edith for a discarded armchair. She would not refuse. Not the stammered plea of an old man living alone with nothing to his name.

He lifted his arm, fired. It was done. Only he had no gun, and the man still lived. Samuel looked away. There were gray circles of condensation on the windowpanes, as though someone had been standing outside, breathing hot air onto the glass while they peered in. For a moment he believed it, believed that the man's family had come now that the island had been claimed as his, believed that they were watching him. He imagined opening the front door, being confronted by their approach: all those bodies from the sinking boat, dripping, sea-tossed, their clothes patchworked with salt, climbing over the walls, hunching up the sandy inclines, across the long yellow grass. And along with them, others more sinister. Skeletons from inside the wall, pushing their way out, causing the rocks to tumble and fall, the whole thing to disintegrate, as they rose and came for him.

Samuel exhaled into the cup of his hand, his breath

thick on his face. He was going mad. It was certain. The dizziness, the fall, the visions of nightmares come to life; all the memories, and the man here. It was making him ill.

He blinked, looking back toward the couch. He saw something then on the coffee table, something he had not noticed when he'd entered the room. The man must have made them by starlight, must have known that he would disturb Samuel if the light had been on. He had taken one of the jars from the charity box, filled it with scraps of blue-and-white paper from the discarded magazines, rolled into little pearls. Then, using the cable ties, buttons, and wire, he had fashioned a bunch of multicolored flowers. They were the marks of an immigrant and refugee, products such as these. Beaded creatures and jewelry, bowls and windmills. Items made with care, and sold for hardly anything at all.

There had been many migrants in the slums when he was growing up. Some of them had been there for years, before his family had arrived. They had married citizens, had borne children. Across the street from where Samuel's family lived was a couple who had fled their country's postindependence civil war, and although he had long since forgotten, he could remember them still as they came out each morning with a blanket and their baskets of wire and beads, so that they could sit in the sunshine as they made their goods. They nodded greetings when Samuel carried his father outside after breakfast. It was his custom to sit on his chair and call to passing children, asking them how school was and whether they swore allegiance each morning to the ornately framed photograph of the president that adorned all shops and schools and public buildings now. He asked if the great man had been to visit them yet, and showed a tatty paper flag he had kept from the inauguration parade, telling them that he hoped to meet him one day, hoped to have the opportunity to shake his hand.

One morning he called to the couple across the road, waved his flag at them, said, "I'm sorry that your story isn't as happy as the one we have in this country, but I'm glad we're able to give you a new and better life here."

The woman smiled, but the man said, "It was like this for us, too, Uncle. I'm sorry to tell you that. We were exactly like you."

Samuel's father laughed. "No, my friend, that isn't possible. This is a free and democratic country. We're independent, we have it all now. There will be no problems here. Your country did it the wrong way, you made mistakes."

"Wait, Uncle. You will see."

"There's nothing to see. You're wrong, neighbor, very wrong."

Even so, he befriended the couple, asked Samuel to carry him across the street, to bring coffee for himself and for them. He sat talking in this way most mornings, and with time began to help them feed beads onto wire, to cut soda cans, fashion cars that children raced in the dusty streets. But he never took money for his work. He did not want it, he said, though their family had little enough as it was. Behind his back, the couple gave money to Samuel's mother. She hid it in an old headscarf and told Samuel, "I'm not too proud to take money from refugees. They're nice people, but let them pay something for being here."

She was not the only one with that sentiment. Independence had not brought the things that had been promised. In fact, many people complained that they had less now than before. "It's all very well and good to have the vote," they would say, "but we can't eat it, can we?" Nor could they eat the new flag, or the national anthem's trumpets and flourish. Resentment began to grow, bitterness for promises not kept began to infect them. Samuel shared in that bitterness. His father was a grinning cripple, a fool who held firm that the president was as good as the Messiah, that one day he would come down into the slums and thank the wounded and bereaved for their services to the country. He took pride in what he believed was his place in history, seeing himself as someone who would mean something to the future. This man who had already been forgotten by his friends in the Movement, and whom people took back alleys in order to avoid, tired as they were of his talking and reminiscing.

By then the General, who would later become the Dictator, was gaining popularity with the masses. He did enter the slums, did spend time with the people, listening to their grievances. When crowds gathered, he talked to them with a booming voice, and when still more gathered, he lifted a bullhorn to his mouth and shouted so that the topmost flats seemed to sway with the reverberations. He spoke to the fears of the people, made promises to them. He blamed foreigners for their suffering, vowed to end their troubles.

"Listen to me if you're hungry, listen to me if you're cold and afraid," he called to them. "I am like you. I know how you feel. Don't let this uniform fool you. Underneath it I am the same as each one of you. We are the ones who fought for independence. We are the ones who fought to have our own nation. We are the ones who lost loved ones, who were imprisoned and wounded. We are the ones who died. Why are we still sharing our country with foreigners after all of that? Let them go back to their own homes and fight for their own freedom. We don't want them here, taking from us, stealing what we fought so hard for. This country is ours, no one else has a right to claim it. No one else has a right to be here. This country is ours alone, only ours. The time has come to make them see that they're no longer welcome. The time has come to make them leave!"

In his speeches he called out the new government and president, claiming they weren't looking after their own first. Did they not care about those who had put them in power with blood and sweat? Did they care nothing for their people? Power made men hateful. Power made men forget everyone but themselves.

It was not a thing that Samuel cared to remember.

Not even with the distance of time was it something that he could return to without shame. How he had taken part in what the General called the culling. Samuel had had no problem with foreigners. But he was a young man, full of anger, and when the surge came in his neighborhood, he was swept up in it. He did not like to think of it afterward, to remember how he had picked up the axe from the woodpile and joined the tumult in the streets. He killed no one that day, though everything he smashed, everyone he chased, was in that moment to blame for his father's naivety, for his ruined body, for their lost home in the valley, and the poverty of their life in the dirty city.

Shame did not come immediately. Not for chasing the friends of his father out of their home, even as they begged him not to, not for smashing their baskets and leaving their beaded creatures lying around as though the products of a dreadful slaughter. He laughed as the woman tripped in the street, as the man pissed himself, as their child gabbled in a foreign tongue. And afterward, when the culling had been subdued, when the bodies and debris had been cleared away, he examined the axe carefully. He knew he had struck nobody with it, yet even so, when he saw a spot of blood on the handle, for several days he walked with his head very high, in the manner of a hero.

Samuel's parents did not guess his involvement in the massacre. If they ever found out, it was not through him. They did wonder at the increasing distance between themselves and their son. There had been difficulties ever since they had come to the city, but he had always taken care to provide for the family. Now he brought home nothing. He rose early, went out, did not return until a few hours before dawn, always emptyhanded. He slept little, rising again, departing.

He left the flat to walk the city, to observe the places left empty by the fleeing or dead. Gone was the pride that he had felt, gone, too, the pleasure in the drop of blood. He was afraid of what he had done, of the destruction he had wrought. He chose to confront the absences, to stare them out, all the while trying to comfort himself that, really, he was not to blame. What had he done, after all? Hardly anything. Almost nothing. He had been little more than a bystander. He was innocent.

He no longer saw his friends, gave up his thieving and loitering. He trod the streets alone, the soles of his shoes wearing thin, until they fell apart and he had to repair them with patches from tires, his appearance comical now beneath his shiny imitation American-style suit. He went always the same route, so that he knew at once when anything altered; he observed the empty places begin to fill as people returned, or new ones came. Within a year it was as though the culling had never occurred. Still, there were differences. The General had already made his move, the president's corpse was rotting in a ditch somewhere, and a band of armed militiamen kept order in public places, enforcing curfews that shortened Samuel's wanderings, and caused people to live in fear.

It was during that time that Samuel first saw Meria. She was among a handful of people that sat around a splintering wooden table at an illegal bar in one of the back streets that he passed. They were there most evenings, about five of them usually, and it was their location that made him notice them. Most people sat at pavement tables in the evening's coolness, looking out for acquaintances, chatting with passersby. But this group sat indoors, showing no interest in anything beyond their table and themselves. He wondered what kept them there, what secrets they held that could not be shared with others.

After a while he began to recognize individual members of the group. Three of them were men. A tall, big man with broad shoulders; a younger one, with a slope to his shoulders; and one with a receding hairline that made his forehead high and bright. The man with the sloping shoulders always sat beside a woman who wore her hair in an Afro, a style that Samuel disliked, so he took a dislike to the woman too. But Meria, she wore her hair shaven, causing the darkness of her face to stand out. At first he thought she was an immigrant, so dark was she, but once he had gotten closer, had seen her eyes, he saw that she was not. Where the other woman wore dresses and jewelry, Meria wore trousers and no adornments. She hunched over her beer, appearing to be angry at all times. When she spoke, she often pointed a finger. She tilted her head a little when she listened.

One evening Samuel entered the illegal bar and ordered a beer. He sat at a small table near the group, his back to them. They spoke low, but he had learned in his years as a thief to listen well. What he heard disappointed him. Their agitated whispers were about the Dictator, about oppression, freedom of speech, all those things that he had heard often enough at meetings with his father.

"Our enemies," Meria was saying, "are the political profiteers, the men who swindle and cheat, who take bribes. They are the people who are little more than ministers of waste, who spend money on making themselves look big, on making the country look big to those overseas, caring nothing that people are starving. What we need is a new order. Those that take bribes and embezzle and are corrupt in any way must be killed. They must be publicly executed, they must be eradicated. That, and nothing else, is the purpose of the People's Faction. Our purpose is to kill."

Despite her views, Samuel was drawn to Meria in a way that he had never been to the various girlfriends he had had around the city. Girls who had slept with him for gifts, or for as little as a drink, girls who liked a man with money, never mind where it came from. The same girls who now, if he happened to pass them in his wanderings, looked at his fading suit and repaired shoes with disgust, pretending not to know him.

It became habit for Samuel to go to the illegal bar to sip at a beer for an hour, listening beside the group. Sometimes Meria's eyes fell on him and she glared, whispering to her companions, until one day she stood up and called, "Look, Suits, are you a spy or not? Arrest us if you're going to or else fuck off."

"No," he said. "I'm not a spy."

"What then, huh? What do you want?"

"I like to listen. That's all. It's interesting."

One of the others, the broad-shouldered man that he had come to know as Big Ro, walked over and shook his hand, invited him to join them.

"You let a man dressed like that sit with us?" Meria said.

Big Ro laughed and pulled out a chair for Samuel. "Don't mind Meria," he said, "she takes a while to warm up to strangers."

The others were welcoming enough, asking his name, where he was from. The girl with the Afro was Keda; her boyfriend, with the sloping shoulders, Selo.

"Keda and I come from the southwest," Selo said. "We're farming people. We talk funny, we know, we have these accents, as Big Ro likes to remind us. But to us, you city people are the ones with the strong accents." He laughed. "Sometimes it's easy to forget that we come from the same country."

"I was from the countryside once," Samuel said. "We were made to leave. Why did you leave?"

Keda said, "We weren't as unfortunate as you. We

chose to come to the city. We've been here eight months, and in the beginning we slept on the streets, we had to do terrible things to survive. But then the People's Faction found us, they helped us. Now we're members, and we help them in our turn."

"Have you ever been to a meeting of the Faction?" asked Juma, the man with the receding hairline.

"I never even heard about them until I met you. I thought all opposition parties were banned."

"Banning something doesn't make it disappear."

"That's true."

"But you don't agree with the idea of fighting against tyranny? You support the Dictator?" asked Big Ro.

"No, I'm not saying that. I know about opposing power. My father was among those who fought for independence."

"That's great," said Juma. "And you? Did you also fight?"

"No, I was too young."

Meria slapped her hand on the table. "It was only a few years ago. You would have been a teenager then. Old enough if you'd believed in it. If you're a coward, then at least be honest about it."

"Meria," said Big Ro.

"I don't have time for cowards," she said.

Afterward, walking with them—he remembered it well, that walk. It was late evening, the streets heavy with traffic, stalls beginning to be packed away before curfew. A soldier had stepped out of a doorway, looking back as he took his leave of someone. Not seeing where he was going, he had collided with Samuel.

"Watch yourself, boy," he had said. Then, "Don't you apologize, boy? Don't you beg my pardon?"

"I'm sorry, sir," he said.

"Damn right you are, boy."

The man moved on, rubbing his hands up and down his shirtfront and sleeves, as though to remove Samuel from them.

The others had walked on, but Meria waited for Samuel. He felt himself blush, and took a moment to choose a swear word he could use to describe the man, almost reaching out a hand to take hers. But then she said, "Oh yes, Suits, I see it now. You're a real tough one. You fight for what you believe in."

He dropped his hand, slunk back, taking a left turn into an alleyway, not saying a word of goodbye.

There was no injury, no bruise even, from the collision, yet Samuel nursed his arm as though there were. He fashioned a sling out of a piece of cloth, held his arm in a rigid triangle. When asked, he told people that he had fallen or been hit by a bike taxi. He avoided the illegal bar and the group, instead obsessively tramping the streets again. He looked for the soldier. He remembered the man's face: a mustache, small teeth, and a dappling of black moles under each eye, so that he appeared at first glance to be ill. Samuel imagined finding him. Imagined how he would walk toward him, filling up the entire pavement, refusing to move, so that the soldier would be forced to step aside, to walk in the street. Or he would run up to him, ram him so hard that he would fall down.

Several times he saw him, and several times he strode toward him, was ready. But, always, he moved aside before the collision, walking away, wishing he had the nerve to take the soldier's head and beat it into the ground, but knowing he did not.

As his failures increased, Samuel removed the sling from his arm. He gave up his searches, returned to the bar. Meria smirked when she saw him.

"You're back, Suits. We heard you'd been injured. Come, sit down. Why don't you show us your terrible scars?"

On an afternoon several months later, it began to rain very hard, as it often did at that time of year. Samuel was in the street, on the way to the illegal bar. He had no umbrella with him, and he rushed toward the nearest shop for cover. His head was lowered as he entered, murmuring a thank-you to the person who held the door open for him. When he looked up it was too late. The soldier was already running across the street, a folded newspaper held over his head.

In the living room, Samuel looked down at where the man lay on the couch. He aimed and shot again, remembering the urge to humiliate someone, to smash their face in, to make them cower.

He left the cottage in haste, the previous day's dizziness returning to him as he crossed the threshold. He put a hand against the leaning tree beside the tower steps and tried to catch his breath. Pulling at the neck of his jersey, he remembered again the finger drawn across a dark throat—only this time the finger cut through flesh, made a slit that caused the head to fall backward, to gape blackly. He spluttered, felt his way to the three stone steps, and sat down, pushing his face upward. The breeze touched him; waves moved lightly against the shore; overhead gulls were flying, mewling. The sound startled Samuel, and in his madness it came to him as the cry of a baby. He wondered whether it was Lesi, here on the island. Was the dead child returning to him?

He had only slept with Meria a few times, always hurriedly, in the dark. Always a secret. "Don't even think about telling anyone about this," she'd said. "Don't you fucking dare." But it was to him that she came when she was pregnant, saying, "It's yours," though they both knew there were other men. He did not mention them. Not when she looked as she did, made small by fear.

"Don't worry about anything," he had said. "It'll be all right." He held her, felt her relax against him, her head on his shoulder. He leaned down a little and kissed her forehead. "I'll take care of you. I'll be a good husband to you. We'll be a family together; the rest doesn't matter now."

That broke the softness, and she pushed away from him. "Christ, you would say that. A man like you. A fucking man like you would take another man's baby and want to marry a woman who can't stand him."

Samuel's father was delighted at the news. To have a grandchild born into independence had been his greatest wish. He spoke of little else when Meria visited, eyeing her growing belly eagerly.

Meria was less excited. She would never stay in the one-room flat beyond ten minutes, refusing to eat or drink anything. She disdained his family with their poverty and begging. His father's shriveled legs. The way his sister fawned over the military men, and was said to be involved with Dog now that he'd become a soldier. Most of all she looked down on the fact that they had taken up the business of their culled neighbors. But instead of fashioning creatures out of beads and wire, they made small national flags, silhouettes of the country, little men in uniform. To branch out with other colors or shapes was not possible. Not when they might be misconstrued and associated with opposition parties—parties that had been banned, hunted down, killed. So they used green and red, black, and the dull khaki of the military.

Sometimes, on their way to meetings, Samuel and his new friends might pass Mary Martha where she sat on a pavement, selling these items. Meria would ignore her, walk on with the group, but one time Samuel stopped to talk.

"Hi, how's it going today?" he asked.

"Don't put your dirty shoes on the blanket."

"Sorry." He stepped back, looked down at where she sat hunched up, chewing on a bit of plastic. "Why don't you come with us? I think you'll like it. The meetings are really interesting."

"Oh yes, I'm sure it must be very interesting spending your days talking about how you're going to save the world, while the rest of us try to earn enough money so that we can buy food to feed you."

"Don't say that. It isn't like that."

"Isn't it?"

Samuel knelt down, picked up a wire and bead soldier. "This is good. Who made it?"

"Who do you think? Our father did."

"Well, it's good."

She picked a bit of dirt off the blanket, flicked it away.

"Do you remember the toys he carved for us when we were living in the valley?"

"No."

"Oh, come on, you must remember. They were wonderful. The lion, and that elephant?"

"I said no. I was a baby. I don't remember that place."

Samuel put down the soldier. "Tell me, have you seen Dog recently?"

"Don't start with that. I'm sixteen years old. I can do what I want."

"I'm only asking. He was my friend, you know."

"I know what he was to you, and I know what he is to you now. It must be nice, your life, judging everyone, doing what you want, having no responsibilities."

"I have responsibilities. I'm responsible to this country—"

"Jesus, Samuel, I don't want to hear that shit. Just fuck off, will you? Fuck off to your meeting and leave me alone."

When Meria visited the flat, she watched his parents at their work, watched his mother smiling, her squint in the dull light.

"We didn't have money to send our children to school," Samuel's mother said. "But your child will have more opportunities. We will work hard to make sure that happens. He will read and write. He will be an educated man and get a good job. Maybe in the bank."

Samuel's father nodded, "Oh yes, and he will have a name to match his good fortune. Freedom or Independence. Something like that, so that each time he speaks his name, he will do so with pride, knowing what his grandfather fought for, knowing that I gave him this gift of freedom from slavery."

That was when Meria could take no more. "Where is your freedom? What did independence bring you? Your generation brought us failure, nothing more. You should have done it properly. You should have obliterated it all, started from the beginning, and not simply tried to repeat what we had before. A corrupt elite, enslaving the poor. The poor must rise up. That is when you will have freedom, only then. Not this crippled existence of scrounging and scrounging and telling yourself that it is what you almost died for. This isn't freedom, and no child of mine will be taught to think that this prison of exploitation is anything other than what it is."

Samuel's father blinked. "You are very angry, girl. If you are not careful, the child will be born with a bitter heart."

"Better a bitter heart than the thoughts of an imbecile."

Yet Meria was soon forced to move in with Samuel's family. She had worked for an agency, translating international news reports from English that were then sold on to national papers. But with increased censorship and growing paranoia, most international news was not allowed through. The agency shut down. She lost her job and could not afford the rent on the flat that she had lived in.

She had always been loud, never afraid to give her opinion or to criticize. Now she became quiet. She tapped her fingers with irritation when people spoke. She gulped down half a beer or pulled hard on a cigarette as though to prevent herself from speaking. She glared at the group when they met. It was perhaps worst at night. Once he woke to find her sitting beside him, her knees drawn up to her chin, smoking, watching Samuel through narrowed eyes.

"What is it?"

"You talk in your sleep, do you know that?"

"Sorry. Am I keeping you awake?"

"No."

"What did I say?"

"Nothing."

They argued, too, in that time. About food. How she would not eat. She blamed it on morning sickness, then on his mother's cooking. It wasn't fit for animals, she said. There were days at a time when she ate nothing at all, others when she chewed a single mouthful for an entire meal.

"You must eat," Samuel said, pushing a plate toward her. Then to frighten her, "Do you want the baby to die?"

"Would it be so bad?"

Later, when the contractions started, and the rush of fluid came, she grabbed his hand, saying, "I can't let this child have a father like you. You have to prove yourself. You have to be more than this."

"How? I don't know what you want from me. What can I do?"

"You have to take the vow. You have to join us properly."

Samuel didn't have a chance to reply. He was ushered from the room by his mother and a neighbor, was left to wait in the street for the birth to take place.

It was the smallest baby he had ever seen. Small and strangely yellow in color. The little fists were clenched, the eyes closed. He held him a while, smelled him, felt the tiny fragility of his body. He knew then what his father had meant about freedom. How it mattered, what it would mean for the little thing. And he said, "Yes, I'll do it. I'll take the vow."

He was sitting like that, holding Lesi while Meria slept, when Juma came. Samuel thought he had come to see the baby, but instead of congratulating him, Juma spoke in hushed tones and called Samuel outside. A body had been found. Samuel was to come.

Samuel followed Juma to an abandoned building site. There were many of them around the city, projects begun under the colonial government and then discarded when independence came. This was not one of those: this was to have been a large orphanage, built by order of the country's first president; this was to have been a home for those who had lost their parents during the fight for independence. The president was to be their father now, the country their mother. A big ceremony had been held to mark the beginning of construction, with cakes handed out to street children, and a banner hung in front of the site, bearing the president's smiling face, his arms open. Yet soon all work stopped. There was talk of funds being embezzled, of the new government being bankrupt. Beyond foundations being dug, and some cement struts being raised, nothing more was done. Soon the site became a dumping ground for the neighborhood. By the time Samuel was called to it, it was perhaps a third of the way full with refuse, though sometimes this was higher, depending on how much it had rained. Rats survived among the rubbish, as did mosquitoes and feral cats.

When Samuel arrived, a man he knew only as Jakes was waiting for them. It was he who had found the body. He stood with his back turned to the pit, his T-shirt pulled up over his nose and mouth. To the side of him was a fresh pile of vomit. The stench of the place was terrible, and Samuel brought his wrist up to his nose as he approached. It was high summer; heat rotted the garbage in the warm water. A cloud of midges hung over it all.

Samuel looked down to where Juma was pointing. Big Ro lay naked, torso upward, one arm bent behind him, the other out to the side, bruises clearly visible. He no longer had a face; it had been beaten from him. But Samuel recognized him by his left foot: all the nails had blackened and fallen off after a soldier had ridden over his foot with a motorcycle the month before. The foot had not been touched under interrogation, and yet it was brutal, hideous, more so than the stain where his face had been.

"Dumped in the night," said Jakes, his mouth moving under the T-shirt so that it took Samuel a moment to understand what he was saying.

"What do you think, Sam?" Juma asked.

"It's him."

"Yes, but how are we going to get him out of there?"

"It will have to be at night, otherwise the police—" said Jakes.

"No. That won't be possible. Not in the dark. It's too dangerous. There's the curfew, and the patrols. They patrol here every night. Do you want us all to end up like that?" said Juma.

"Burn him?"

"In all that water?"

In the end, they borrowed a cart from Jakes's uncle who had once had a grocery stall at the market. One of the wheels pulled to the right, the other squeaked, but it did the job. They pushed it through the streets, collecting refuse from neighboring houses, slums, stalls, pavements. When the cart was full, they went to the site, took a pole and pulled the body closer, before dumping the contents of the cart over him. Five times they filled the cart and dumped it before they felt satisfied that he would not be uncovered.

"It isn't much of a burial," Juma said, making the sign of the cross.

"It's more than many have had," Samuel replied. He wiped his forehead, put a hand over his mouth. Somewhere in the creases of his fingers still lingered the smell of newborn baby.

He moved away from the cottage, across the yellow grass of the headland, thinking at first to go down to the jetty, to inspect the fallen stone wall. But he went up instead, along the slope that narrowed toward the eastern end of the island. It rose as it thinned, forming a little peak at its farthest reach. Here someone had at one time erected a squat beacon—a small cement pillar upon which a metal cross, or something of that sort, had once stood. Now only the upright remained. Samuel picked at the rusting pole, and held on to it as he peered down to the small eastern shore that he rarely visited.

The waves were gentle, the tide low. He could make out rock pools, seaweed, the tiny curls of shells. But there was something else. He put a hand over his eyes and told himself that it was a seal, that it could be nothing more, though he knew, had seen easily enough, that it was human.

For a moment he considered returning to the cottage, fetching the man to help him recover the body.

Why not, after all? Why not, when the man was young and strong? He looked back across the island. The cottage was some distance away. The front door was open, and he wondered if it was he himself who had left it like that. Or had it been the man? Had he risen, left the cottage? Was he out here now, looking for Samuel? Once more he remembered the finger, the rush of fear in the dark.

The cove below was hard to reach, a difficult descent, steep and rocky. The man would not know to look there, would not know that it existed. It would be a good place for Samuel to hide.

She was lying on her back, her dress up over her hips. She wore no underwear. Samuel pulled the dress down before he did anything else. Her eyes were open, as was her throat. There was a wide gap where it had been cut. All night, all morning, that finger across the throat, and now here the line was, clean as something in a butcher's window.

He bent a little and looked at the woman's face. Her hair was braided close to her scalp, her ears stuck out slightly. She had similar cheekbones to the man, the same narrow jaw and wide mouth. Had they both come from the boat that he had seen on Winston's phone? They must have done. But why would a drowning man take the time to slit a woman's throat? Perhaps that was what he had come into Samuel's room to say the previous night. It had not been a threat, it had been a confession—he had killed a woman, and had fled. He was not a refugee at all. He was a fugitive. No wonder he hadn't wanted to be taken to the mainland.

What might the man do if he discovered that Samuel had the body? He was a murderer. Already he wanted Samuel gone. Already he had tripped him, had begun to take over the cottage. He might do anything else, anything, if he knew about the body. But to bury the woman would take time, time that Samuel did not have. Not if the man had risen, if he was in fact out on the island, searching for Samuel.

The eastern shore was backed by a brake of low trees that grew on the shaded side of the drop from the peak. Within the brake was an old stone hut, largely hidden from view. There was no path leading to it, nothing to mark its presence. When he'd first arrived on the island, Samuel would not have known of its existence if his predecessor hadn't pointed it out to him. They had been standing at the beacon and Joseph had said, "There was a ruin in there, you know. I haven't been there in years. Maybe it's collapsed and all gone by now."

"What was it?"

"Some kind of blockhouse, I suppose, from some or other war."

"What war?"

"Oh, you know, one of those the colonizers fought over land and slaves. Something like that."

Samuel had climbed down, pushed through the growth until he reached the tumble of the hut. Its walls had crumbled, half the roof had fallen in. Inside were rotten wooden crates, empty bottles, rusted tins. Black words and images, scrawled in charcoal, filled the walls.

Later, when the island became his, he cleared the bushes and weeds from around the hut, removed the trash, packed the loose stones into piles. He swept up the bird shit, the feathers, the abandoned nests. In the dirt of the floor he found several empty rifle cartridges, a coin he did not recognize, and the shell of a tortoise. In all his years on the island that was the only sign of a tortoise he had ever seen. He wondered if the population had been eaten by smugglers and sailors, or whether it had been a pet of one of the slavers who had sailed these waters in the past, left behind to live on the island alone, and to die here, forgotten.

The woman was thin. Shorter than the man, and lighter too. Samuel grabbed her ankles and pulled her over the damp sand. Her dress hiked up over her hips again. He looked away and continued pulling. She moved easier than the man had done, her ascent up the shore quick and uncomplicated. Only when he reached the pathless slope to the brake did it become more difficult. He had to push the tall, sharp bushes out of the way with his backside. She jolted over the uneven surface, while scrub sprang up between her naked thighs.

It had been many years since he had last been to the hut, and he found it now overgrown, the entrance blocked by a large thorny bush. Samuel first had to leave the woman, taking care again to pull her dress down over her thighs. His thumb brushed against her and he stammered an apology. A little brown bird watched from the roof of the hut, but flew off when he bent down and put his hand on the trunk of the bush, making the top branches with their hard gray leaves rustle. There was only a thin layer of soil on the stone floor, so that the roots were shallow, spread wide. They lifted out easily.

He leaned the bush against the outside wall and stepped inside the hut. In places where enough sand had accumulated or where cement had weathered, a few shrubs grew. They were smaller than the one from the doorway, stunted by the dark interior. Otherwise it was much as he had left it. The piled rocks, the falling roof, the tortoise shell. It was lying on the floor, upside down. He picked it up. A few of the plates were missing; the inside was brown with dirt. He blew on it, wiped it down with his sleeve, then put it on top of one of the stone piles.

He returned to the woman, pulling her across the threshold and over to a section of the hut where walls and ceiling were still intact. He neatened her, closed her eyes with clumsy fingers. He wondered for a moment if he should say a prayer, though he had never prayed for the ones that had come before.

He did not like to leave her yet, and crouched unsteadily beside her, wishing he had a handkerchief or something to wrap around her throat and bind her wound. He thought of what was to come: of covering her with stones. He remembered again Big Ro's burial, the stink of it. Two murders. Two murders, and Samuel the undertaker for both. What had he done, what could he have done about either of them? He felt the answer rise up in his chest. These memories, these memories, hunting him down, taking possession of him. These memories, and a word now, just a word remembered, that moved inside him, sat on his tongue, waiting there, until he spoke it out loud. He turned his face toward the woman, bent down to her, said, "Violence."

After the murder of Big Ro, the group became more involved in the People's Faction. Where they had previously been on the outskirts, mostly posturing, they now became fervent in their membership. They went to regular meetings, passed worn paperbacks among them in which they read theories of how to create a better world and life. They recited quotes from the texts, argued over words and phrases. At the meetings they rose, made speeches.

"Violence! That is the answer. When we, all of the people, agree to violence, when we have educated others about the need for it, that is when we will begin to triumph. We will no longer be under the thumb of anyone. We will be dominated by no one," said Selo.

Meria agreed, pointing with a cigarette as she spoke. "Blood will be our cement. With it we will build a new nation. A strong one. Too many of us have lived in shadows, feeling ourselves to be worthless. It's only when we fight and shed blood that the power will finally be ours."

They demanded to know what Samuel thought, pressing him to share their views. "Will you take arms?" they asked. "Will you embrace violence and fight?"

"The Independence Movement didn't rely on violence and they succeeded," he said.

"Succeeded?" said Meria.

"Yes."

"Wasn't it violence that crippled your father? Violence must be answered with violence. Maybe if he had known that then he would not be such a burden to his people now. If he had only had the guts to fight."

On a night soon after the birth of Lesi, Samuel dressed in a gray T-shirt and a pair of baggy shorts. He went barefoot. He removed the gold chain from around his neck, and took off the wristwatch that he was so proud of. He allowed Meria to blindfold him, and then to guide him into the midnight-quiet street where he could hear a car engine running. He knew that the lights would be off, that there was to be no talking—nothing to alert the soldiers to their presence. He was assisted by two sets of arms into the backseat; finding it already full, he had to perch on the thighs of another man and poke his head out the window.

The car was Juma's. He recognized the coughing motor, the way the backseat jolted as it went over potholes. He estimated that there were five or six of them in the back, two in the front passenger seat. He could hear their tense breathing, throats being cleared awkwardly. In the front the driver burped, and though his head was outside, Samuel could smell the onions and beef on Juma's breath. He had had to fast for two days before the vow, and now he was hungry and his mouth was dry.

The journey seemed to be a long one. He had known it would be, that they would be taken far outside the city. When the car eventually stopped, Samuel's thighs were cramping, he was sweating, and increasingly nauseous from hunger and the lurching motion. Someone led him from the car and walked him through long wet grass; the sound of night insects was loud around him. Then the blindfold was removed and he blinked out into a darkness that eventually revealed within it other blinking men and women. There were a dozen of them, perhaps more. A woman Samuel did not know stood in front of them holding a burning torch. Selo walked along the semicircle of newcomers and handed each of them a stick. One by one they were invited to approach the woman and to light their torch from hers. Afterward, they followed her to a large pile of soil beneath a tree. Each of the newcomers took a handful, then stood in a circle around the pile. They brought the soil up to their lips with their right hands and took a small amount of it into their mouths before swallowing.

"What is this?" the woman said, pointing at the pile.

Together they recited the vow as they had been taught to do in the preceding days:

"This is the land. I have tasted it. It is in my blood. It is my body and my body is it. I vow to the land without fear. If I die, then I will return to the land and be born again. I vow with blood and with fire, for the land is mine and I am the land."

In the island's stone hut, Samuel grew restless with memory. He could feel the burning torch in his hand, wet grass on his legs. He walked up and down, stamping his feet. The woman's body shifted a little at his stamping, and he turned away, not wanting to see her move. Then he knelt down and scratched at the thin layer of dirt on the stone floor until he held a small amount in his hand. He brought it to his mouth, licked it with a dry tongue, and murmured, "The land is mine. I am the land."

The wind was up, and it whipped against him as he left the hut, climbing slowly back up to the narrow peak. At the top, he paused to catch his breath. Dry grass rattled at his knees. The sun was weak, the sky cloudy; it would rain in the afternoon.

Down on the southern shore something was moving, black against the grit and pebbles. It was the man. He had taken a jacket and woolen hat from the hallway, and was walking up and down the beach, looking at the sand. From time to time he stopped, nudged something with his foot, or bent down to pick it up and examine it. Then he moved on to the rock pools and boulders, searching among them too.

Samuel wondered what he was looking for. It had to be the woman, surely. Proof of his crime. But to look for her in such a way—as though she were no more than an item fallen from his pocket.

The man rose from where he had been kneeling and scanned the island headlands. For half a minute his gaze rested on the beacon behind which Samuel was crouching. Then he moved up the beach, away from the water. Soon he was out of sight, and Samuel had to come out from behind the beacon and peer down. It took him a moment to find the man again. He was standing at the stone wall, his hands on it. Then he began to lift individual stones, raise them above his head, as though testing their weight.

The man was preparing to kill him.

He had come armed on the day of the march, his weapon an old cricket bat that he had found as a boy. It was pocked from hitting stones, and the face had a long crack in it that he had tried to fix with tape. Beside him Meria carried a broom handle, Keda a length of knotted rope, while Juma and Selo had polo mallets from the dumping ground behind the old colonial club. Others had come with tools, bricks and rocks, broken scrap that had weight or an edge.

The agreement was to aim for the statue at the far end of the square. It was fifteen feet tall, carved out of black marble, and depicted the Dictator's head and the top part of his torso. The shoulders and peaked hat had been made unnaturally broad in order to balance the massive head. Even so, it was an idealized version of him—a younger, thinner man. For he was fat, had jowls and chins that had earned him the nickname Bullfrog behind his back.

The marchers each knew the statue, had seen it before, had walked beneath it or within view of it, this thing that watched them at all hours, that seemed to know their thoughts and deeds. It was the face of tyranny, a monster that followed their steps, hunted them, sentenced them to death. Now was the time to forget books and meetings and words. They would act. They would topple the head, bring down the monster. Now was the time for violence. All else would follow.

"Make him fall!" they shouted. "Make him fall!"

Within that riot, Samuel could not hear his own voice, so loud was the noise around him. His mouth seemed to gape, making no sound at all. He continued though, feeling that all the voices were rising up out of his own lungs. These voices that occupied everything, they represented so much more than the Faction and its members. Surely there were more than a million people present. Surely the whole country had come. They were all there, every person, all of them, marching to bring down the Dictator.

In the distance came the sound of rifle fire, but Samuel was not afraid. The march could not be stopped. Not this tide of men and women who would no longer be told how to live. They had given up fear. They knew only strength.

Only afterward, in the first interrogation room, did he learn that the march had been poorly attended, with little more than two thousand people participating. The event had barely disrupted the peace, and though hundreds had died and many more were arrested, it had made no impact at all. There was nothing reported about it locally, nothing in the international press. And before too long the march became less than a myth, a mostly forgotten rumor, too faded to bear repeating.

But at the time, they had felt invincible. They had not known that they were no more than a handful. When they reached the statue, the attack was frantic. Samuel hit out with his bat. Others did the same with their weapons. Meria's broom handle snapped in half and she began to stab at the statue's collar with the splintered end, yelling, "Now, now, now!" Soon afterward Samuel's bat fell apart in his hands, and he threw it aside and scrambled up the smooth face of the Dictator, using the grooves in the lips and the dusty cleft of the chin to haul himself up. Once he was standing on the top lip, Samuel hit at the cheek with his bare fists. It would fall. He would make sure of it.

A few protesters stood on the flat top of the hat, one of them perched on the visor. On either side people were hanging from the Dictator's earholes, and beside Samuel a girl bit at one of the nostrils. On the ground, people clawed to get ahold of the head. Many were too far back to touch the statue and had taken to throwing things, regardless of the people they might hit. They hurled bottles and shoes, spanners, fruit, shit, and stones. One of the men on the hat was struck and fell down onto the closely packed crowd, floating on top of them for several moments before he was noticed and helped down. Despite all this, the statue did not yield.

Then the soldiers were upon them and people began to scatter. Shots were fired. The marchers were attacked with cudgels, beaten, and trampled. There was blood on the cobbled ground as people dropped and screamed. To Samuel it did not seem possible—not when the head still had to fall. There could be no attack on them until it was gone. By then he had found an axe somewhere, and he had moved from the lip, was beside one of the shoulders, swinging at it. In the square, soldiers were herding the protesters. From where he stood, Samuel could see the ring of uniformed men, could see their steady aiming and firing as they packed the people tight until there could be no escape from the rifles and truncheons. But Samuel would not be taken so easily. He would not allow himself to be. "I fear no violence!" he shouted, and threw himself from the statue, landing on the back of a soldier. "The land is mine!"

The soldier fell beneath him, and they rolled on the ground, grappling with each other. But Samuel was stronger, he was able to sit on the man's chest and to pin down his arms with his knees. He took the soldier by the throat and began to choke him, watching as he spluttered, as his face swelled and reddened. For a moment Samuel thought it was that other soldier beneath him, the one who had humiliated him before. He squeezed down, pressed until he was certain something would give way, seeing in the action the extinction of the man, but not only him, of all the humiliations he had ever suffered, all of the men and women who had mocked him.

Samuel could feel his mind darkening, his lungs thin with the effort. The soldier would die. He would be dead. Somewhere—was it nearby or was it a memory?—he heard a cry: "Violence and blood!" He pushed down with his knees, held tight, until the soldier's lips began to purple, spit to froth at the corners of his mouth.

Samuel weakened his grip. He could not stand it— the look of the soldier's face—could not stand to have it in front of him; not the way the neck felt in his hands, not the way his lips rolled and foamed, not the way his fingers clawed at Samuel's legs. He let go and sat back, watching as the soldier opened his eyes, gasped for breath. He had not killed him. The man lived.

Samuel made his way down toward the northern end of the headland. He went the long way around so that the man would not see him, would not guess where he had been and what he had hidden. He came to the crumbling jetty. A plastic shopping bag gripped one of the wooden uprights. Usually Samuel would have walked to the edge with a stick and removed the bag, but today he only looked at it hanging wetly where it ought not to have been. It seemed a hundred years since he had last been here. A century within which he had trebled, quadrupled in age. He was older now; very old; older than any man had ever been. His body was in pain, as were his bones. His mind hurt to think of anything other than home and bed. He could capture nothing, everything had become intangible, a dream. There was no man on the island. There was no one but himself. He was alone.

Yet he knew that wasn't true. He caught hold of the man again in his mind, forced himself to remember him.

The threat of him. Would he be able to avoid death for a fortnight, keep alive until the supply boat returned, then flee to the jetty, beg to be let on board, hurrying them to start the motor, to go, to make haste? The island, the tower, the cottage, the wall, and his vegetables. All of it would be left behind, to be taken over and ruled by this other man. The smotherweed would be allowed to grow wild. It would cover the buildings, the garden, the land. The stone perimeter would collapse as the sea moved in, carving away the island, making away with it, until nothing remained at all.

He could not allow that to happen. He would not give up his land; he would not leave; he would never leave. The land was his always.

He returned to the cottage; the front door stood open still. The wind was picking up. Outside the grass was blown flat. Inside, the pages of magazines were flapping where they sat on the coffee table and bookcase. He knew he would need to return to the garden, to ensure that the plants were securely staked. He would have to pick what could be rescued before the wind jostled everything, knocking the produce to the ground where it would get bruised and damaged by the coming storm.

He wondered whether there was time for a cup of tea first. A sweet one, as he had no energy after his exertions. A slice of bread, a cup of tea, and then outside again. That was what he would do. But then he heard the sound of water in the kitchen, water running without any thought for the rainwater tank and its limited supply. He went forward, stopping in the doorway when he saw the table laden with freshly washed vegetables. The man was at the sink, washing more. There was water all over the counter, on the table, darkening the cement-gray floor.

"What are you doing?" Samuel said.

The man looked up and smiled, waving with his left hand, splattering more water onto the floor as the tap ran and ran.

Samuel moved forward and closed the tap. Then he picked up the tatty brown dish towel and began wiping down the counter. The man spoke, his voice loud. He pointed at the vegetables on the table, then at himself. Samuel clicked his tongue. The man had picked too much. Not everything was ripe enough that it had needed picking; some of it could have been left a day or two, he thought, forgetting the approaching storm. The man continued to talk as Samuel knelt down to wipe the wet splashes on the floor. As he spoke, he took the pot from the sideboard and, as easily as if the cottage and its contents belonged to him, opened the cutlery drawer and took out the knife.

Samuel no longer thought about the previous night's threat of a cut throat. He thought only of that word he had spoken down in the stone hut: violence—though now he uttered another word altogether, "Mine." He stood up from where he had been kneeling. And again, "Mine" as he grabbed the knife out of the man's hand. "Mine, mine, mine!"

The man cried out a little, brought both hands up in front of his chest. Samuel held the knife out toward him. The man backed away through the living room and out the front door as Samuel went after him. When he had crossed the threshold, Samuel slammed the door and shouted, "It stays closed! From now on it stays closed!"

He returned to the kitchen and took out the old wooden chopping board. He began cutting the vegetables roughly, with each slice seeing the knife entering the man's body, putting an end to him.

On those evenings when his niece and nephew had kept the door locked against his entry, Samuel did not always sit outside in the corridor, waiting for his sister to return. Often, he would take his weary legs back out into the city, walk the streets as he had done so many years before, after the culling. He passed through the old neighborhoods, looking for places from his youth, places he might recognize.

The cinema where he'd been given the name American no longer existed. In its place stood a twenty-four-hour gas station with a brightly lit shop in which cool drinks and crisps were sold. The attendants wore red-and-yellow uniforms, and whistled as they filled tanks, washed windows. Across the way was a parking garage; beside that, on a section of what had been the public park, another building was close to completion. Samuel was looking up at the height of it, when the night watchman came out of his little cubby and said, "Fancy, isn't it?"

"What is it?"

"This? It's going to be a mall—you know, like a shopping complex. Four of the levels will have shops on them, one will be only for food and restaurants, stuff like that, one will have an ice-skating rink and play area, and one level, the one right at the top, that's for the VIPs, all the fancy people who park their helicopters up on the roof."

"Helicopters?"

"The whole lot is being built by some oil sheikh from the Middle East or somewhere. When it's done, he wants it all painted gold, inside and out. People are going to have to wear sunglasses just to get near it."

"What about the park?"

"Well, yes, that is sad, yes, but there's still some of it left. And this has brought a lot of jobs, you know. That's what the country needs now. And there's investors now, you know, now that . . . well, now that the situation is different, politically, I mean, after all that stuff that came before."

"Yes, I understand."

"Hey, you aren't looking for a job, are you? No offense, I mean, it just looks like you might be, 'cause, you know, I can have a word if you like. They need some cleaners once it's open."

"Here?"

"Where else?" he laughed, then, seeing the way Samuel was looking at the building, he spoke kindly, "Hey man, is this your first time in the city?"

"No, I grew up close to here, but I've been gone a long time."

"Oh," said the man. He stopped smiling. "Do you mean, you're one of those? Those ones they've been releasing?"

"Yes. That's what I mean."

"Listen, man, this job, I don't think . . . I mean, they won't want trouble here. It's a fancy place. They don't want trouble and problems and all of that."

"No, I understand."

"Things are different now. There's no room for trouble, you see. We just want to live our lives. We don't need to start anything. Everything is good now."

"Don't worry. There'll be no trouble. You've been kind, but don't worry, I'm going now. Thank you."

Despite the intervening years, the city's slums had not improved. In fact, they had grown, spread wide through neighborhoods they had never previously touched. Shacks filled streets, and nothing that Samuel had once known was recognizable. The block of flats where he had lived with his family was covered in graffiti and had lost most of its windows. Between the buildings and shacks, pathways were piled with waste. There was nowhere to tread without stepping in it.

Samuel walked uneasily through the smell and noise. Though he had been away for many years, in his mind nothing had altered outside of the prison. His son was a baby, his sister a teenager, their home the same, everyone still living. The streets continued to be dangerous places in which people rushed from point to point, their heads down, fearful of soldiers. But this place, the city as it had become, this was not anything he knew. Not the motorcycles and cars, more cars than he had ever imagined possible; not the night markets and stalls, or people drinking after dark. Freedom came to Samuel as something he feared, and he walked with care, listening, watching, expecting at any moment to find a rifle in his face, to be told he had committed an offense. To be returned to the Palace where he would be left to live out his days. But there were no soldiers. They had all gone. There were no restrictions now.

Even so, the Dictator had not wholly left. He remained on rusted billboards in the worst areas, the posters so faded and curling with age that he was no more than an outline, a scrap of paper. But Samuel remembered what the boards had shown, the man with his round smiling face, his expressions of paternal love, of command and omniscience. His calls for devotion and adulation. That great face across the city, observing everything, never blinking. To interfere with the posters had been treason, and so they had never been touched, not even now when it was safe to do so, when everything else seemed to have been marked and written upon in shades of filth.

Guilt and shame kept Samuel from seeking out farther places. He could not face the bar where he had met with his comrades, could not go toward the block where Meria had lived, or the culvert where one night they had made love, his knees scraping against the brick wall while she hissed, "Faster, hurry up, hurry." Perhaps out of everything it was the square he felt least able to see again. The giant statue was gone, he knew, it had been removed soon after the Dictator had succumbed at last to the poison one of his advisers had been feeding him for weeks. He had been an old man by then, his paranoias extensive. Behind his back people whispered about the possibility of dementia, of his weakening mind, but his body remained strong, lingering all that time, ever threatening to improve and rise from his sick bed.

Even though the statue was no longer there, Samuel did not wish to return to the site of his failure. If he had killed that soldier, he wondered, if he had had the courage to choke the man to the end, or to have picked up any of the weapons lying nearby, brought it down on his head, smashed him into unconsciousness, what might he have been then? A free man perhaps. A man with a family. Someone better than a frightened informant who had given up the mother of his child to his interrogators. Someone who had had a son to raise, grandchildren to play with. That was what Samuel asked himself as he walked the streets at night. What might he have been if he had been braver, if he hadn't been afraid of murder?

When the sky broke with the afternoon storm, the man had yet to return. Samuel had already been out twice. Once, when the first raindrops had fallen, to put the chickens back in their coops, and again a little later to make sure the light was running smoothly in the tower. The rain was falling hard by then, the view of the sky from the tower solid gray. There was no way of telling where the man might have gone.

Samuel stood at the window for a long time, thinking of the woman lying half naked in the hut. She had been damp from the water when he had dragged her there. He ought to have dried her off, ought to have taken a blanket to cover her up. He did not like to think of her lying on the ground, the rain coming in through the collapsed walls and ceiling, forming puddles that might engulf her, soak into her, make her rot.

The cottage was empty when he returned. The man had not come back. Samuel stirred a pot of stew on the stove, checked that the windows were closed. He took a towel and pressed it against the living room window where rain was coming in through a gap. In his bedroom, he placed a bucket to catch drops from a leak in the ceiling. He did not eat when the food was ready. He boiled water. He sat on the couch, hands on his thighs. He looked at the jar of button flowers on the coffee table.

Later, when there was a knock at the front door, he went to open it, pulling the soaking man into the hallway.

"You didn't have to run away like that," he said. "I'm an old man. Who have I ever hurt?"

He mostly kept his wanderings to the slums and streets of his childhood, but sometimes he went as far as the harbor. On one of these nights he passed a woman leaning against the wall of a fish-packing plant. She called to him, "Want a good time, honey? Come on over and have a taste." Prostitutes were common on the harbor grounds, waiting for fishermen to come in from successful hauls, or foreign sailors to dock. Samuel glanced at the woman, shook his head. He would have continued walking, but he recognized something in her.

"Meria," he said.

"Who's that?" she replied, squinting into the shadows. He walked toward her and she looked surprised, then laughed. "Jesus, you still alive, Suits? I thought you'd died years ago."

"No, I'm still alive."

She had grown solid since he had last seen her. She filled the short dress she was wearing, her breasts pouring out of the top. Her face was hard and ugly, her eyes narrow under a cheap wig. She was missing a few teeth so that she spoke now with a slight lisp.

"Are you just out of prison too?" he asked.

"Nah, I never went."

"No? They didn't get you? Not even afterward?"

She shrugged. "What can I say? I'm clever. I got away."

"How have you been?"

"What do you think? How do I look like I've been, huh?"

"Sorry, I only meant . . ."

"Same old Suits. You'll never change, will you. You got a cigarette?"

He shook his head. Then, "You didn't look up my parents or Mary Martha. She said she never saw you after the march."

"So what?"

"You left Lesi. He was only a little baby and you didn't ever go back for him. We all thought you had to be dead to have done that."

"Well, you were wrong. Here I am, alive and kicking."

"Didn't you wonder what had happened to me?"

She didn't reply, shivered, tried to pull her small jacket across her chest.

"Lesi died, you know," he said.

"I heard."

"You don't seem upset about it."

"Ah, fuck, Suits. It was a long time ago. I have other

problems now. I can't carry that around with me too. Anyway, he was more your child than he was mine. It's better that he died. He'd never have become much of anything."

"You think I'm nothing," he said, moving closer, pointing a finger at her. "You've always thought that. Well, look at you. What are you, Meria, whoring yourself on the docks?"

"Get your fucking finger out of my face," she said. "What have I got to be ashamed of? I fought for my country and now I'm here. So what? What does any of it matter?"

Samuel dropped his hands to his sides and spoke softly. "What about the others? Do you ever see any of them? Do you know what happened to them?"

"Nah, that was all a long time ago. I can't be bothered to remember."

"Well, okay," he said, getting ready to move on. "I guess that's it."

"Listen," she said, looking around. "Do you have any money? Help me out, won't you? I've got kids to feed. Give me something, whatever you got. You owe me that much."

He took the little money he had out of his pocket and held it out to her. She took it eagerly, counting it in her open palm. "Jesus, Suits, I'm not going to suck your cock for a few fucking coins."

"No, that's not what it's for. Anyway, it's all I have. I don't have anything else. I'd give you more if I had it."

She looked him up and down. "You would, wouldn't you? That's true. You were always a pushover."

Laughter sounded, and voices harsh in the still night. They both glanced along the dock. A group of sailors was approaching.

"Listen, Suits, great seeing you and all, but shove off, will you. I need to earn some money tonight."

"Right. Look after yourself," he said, turning away.

He went again to the harbor a few times, with food or coins he had made begging, but he did not see her. He asked other girls about her. They shook their heads, knew nothing, turned away from him, this aged man and his stink of poverty.

He was kind to the man, making up for his earlier behavior with extravagances he would not normally have considered. He led him into his bedroom, took clean clothes from the cupboard, and dry towels, leaving them on the foot of the bed. Then he went into the kitchen and filled a bucket with water he had been keeping hot. He carried it into the room, and left, allowing the man to wash and dress there undisturbed.

When the man came out, smelling of soap and heat, wearing the ill-fitting clothes, Samuel took him through to the kitchen, which was warm from cooking. He handed the man a cup of strong tea, heavy with sugar, and dished up a plate of food for him, taking for himself the chipped plate that had come with the charity items the previous day.

The two men ate in silence. Samuel watched him carefully. From time to time he stretched out his fingers as though they were stiff, or twitched his shoulders to dispel a cold shiver down his back. He ate slower than he had on previous days, taking time to chew. He kept his eyes on the plate in front of him, or straight ahead, at a place on the wall behind Samuel. He did not try to talk. He did not smile.

Samuel looked down, pushing food onto his spoon. When he looked up again the man had turned his head a little, so that he was facing the counter, looking at something. Samuel followed the man's gaze. It was the knife, sitting at the edge of the counter, an arm's length away from the man. He turned to face the man and met his eyes. The man did not blink. He stared back at Samuel, his jaw moving as he chewed.

Suddenly the wind pushed the small kitchen window open. Samuel, startled, jumped up and, reaching past the net curtain, pulled it shut. He took advantage of the disruption to move some items around on the counter: he put the pot in the basin, wiped down the surface, and he moved the knife, too, bringing it closer to where he sat so that it might be in easy reach should he need it.

When he sat down again, he saw that there was something in the middle of the table that had not been there before. He saw poorly at night, and had to lean in close to determine what it was. The shape came into focus before him. His fingers trembled on the table edge. It was the tortoise shell from the stone hut. It could be no other.

The man had found the hut, had gone inside and seen the body. He knew that Samuel had discovered his crime.

Samuel lifted his eyes cautiously. The man raised his hand, extended a finger. Samuel waited to see the slit throat again, but it did not come. This time the finger went to the man's mouth, followed by lips pursed to make a soft sound: "Shhh."

The Fourth Day

When he woke, Samuel was still holding the knife. His hand and arm were stiff. He sat up and moved his shoulder, rolling it a little to remove the tension from it. He put the knife down on the mattress and stretched his fingers as he yawned, felt around his mouth with his tongue, and yawned again.

From outside came familiar sounds. Metal on rock, blow after blow being struck in a slow rhythm. That must have been what had woken him. He got up and walked across to the window and moved aside the net curtain. He could see a part of the outhouse wall, wet grass and rock, gulls in the sky. He dressed quickly, putting on the same clothes that he had worn the previous day, still a little wet in places from when he had run to and from the tower in the rain. He picked up the knife again and gripped it tight, his palm damp.

In the living room he saw that the man's blanket had been neatly folded and put over the back of the couch. The curtains were all open, windows partway open too.

Yet as he reached the hallway, he saw that the front door had been closed. The man had taken heed the day before. Samuel reached for the handle. The door stuck, as it always did, more so in wet weather. He had to lean against it, shuffle the handle, and raise it before the door could be opened inward. It was only as it swung toward him that he realized the key was not in place. He never used it, it had never worked as far as he knew, but he always left it in the lock, and now it was gone. The man had taken it. Here it was. Unmistakable. Here was proof that an attempt was being made to imprison him. Proof that the man planned to lock him up, to take the island for himself.

The island. The island. The island belonged to Samuel. It was his and his alone. He was the one who had tasted the soil down in the hut, he was the one who had molded and tamed and built the place to be what it was. It would not be taken from him; it was time to face the man. He had shown enough kindness, given the man more than enough, much more than others would have done. Now he would confront him, tell him that he could stay until the boat returned, and not a moment longer. Until then, he could sleep on the couch, wear the clothes he'd been given, eat what was put in front of him. There would be no more wandering around the island, no more coming into Samuel's room, no more threats and fingers, no more touching and taking. At the end of the fortnight he was to leave and never to think of returning. He was not welcome.

In the yard, the chickens were eating grain as Samuel approached. The man had let them out, fed them. The little red hen had been let out too. She sat near the man's feet, her bald chest and rump scabbed and goose-pimpled. Her eyes were closed, and she showed no fear at the sledgehammer being swung just a few steps from her. The blows fell heavily, breaking the rock easily. Already a pile of smaller stones had begun to form.

The man had taken the sledgehammer from the hallway without asking. He had taken shoes and a wide-brimmed floppy hat too. The laces of the shoes had not been tied, and they dragged, wet and thick with sand. Five large rocks were lined up nearby. The wheelbarrow was nowhere in sight. Had he carried them up here, using nothing but his arms, this thin, stinking savage? It didn't seem possible to have done in a couple of hours what would have taken Samuel days.

For a moment, as the man added to the pile, Samuel wondered what the stones were for. There were too many for repairs to the wall. Far too many. Then he remembered the woman, remembered that the man had found the hut and the tortoise, that he had found her. He was going to bury her, hide his crime by adding her to the wall somewhere. Still, even for that there were too many stones. A body didn't need that many to be covered, not one of her size. If there had been two bodies, that would have been different, he could have understood it then. There were enough rocks for two bodies.

Samuel closed his eyes, saw again the empty lock of

the front door, the finger across the throat, the same finger against the man's lips. Samuel would be the other body. The man would lock him up inside the cottage, starve him, and beat him until he tired of having a prisoner, and then he would slit his throat, letting blood flow over the faded carpet, staining the sand grains black. Both of them, the woman and himself, would be buried inside the stone wall. There they would decay, their bodies taken up by the dirt, the man's sins becoming part of the island.

The man looked up from his labor, pushed the hat back, and saw Samuel watching. He was sweating heavily, but had not taken off his T-shirt and jersey. He wiped one of the sleeves across his forehead. The sweat stayed on the cheap wool in a line of gray moisture. The man began to walk toward Samuel in greeting, but stopped when he saw that he was carrying the knife. He stilled the smile that had been starting to form, lifted the sledgehammer a little, so that he was holding it two-handed, across his stomach and hips. He moved forward.

Samuel brought up the hand clutching the knife and held it out in front of him, making sure that the blade was at an angle and clearly visible.

The man came closer. He jerked his head at the knife, asked a question in a strong, hard voice. Samuel jerked his own head. "You think I'm some old fool and that I don't know what you're planning. I know you. I know all about you. This old fool knows what you've done and knows what you're planning to do." He pointed with the knife. "Put that down. I'm telling you, I'm not giving the island to you. Put down the hammer. You can't have it. None of it is for you."

The man stood still, stared at Samuel. Samuel moved forward. He shook the knife, said, "Put it down. Go on, put it down."

The man's grip tightened. He frowned.

"I'm telling you to put it down. This is my land. I'm not giving it up."

At last the man shrugged a little, took a step back. He held the sledgehammer out in front of him and let it drop to the ground. Then he raised his hands, palms open, stepping back farther.

For a while they remained like that, their gazes locked. Behind them the chickens clucked, kicked dirt. A cormorant landed on the vegetable garden's stone wall, felt beneath a wing with its beak, flew off again.

The man began to speak softly. He kept his hands up, his eyes on Samuel.

"What are you saying? You know I can't understand you. What are you saying?"

The man took a step forward. Samuel prodded the air with the knife. "Keep back. Don't try it. I'm ready for you."

But the man took another step, continued to speak, his words low. He shook his head a little, curled one half of his mouth into a smile. He proceeded forward slowly: with each step the dirty laces dragged in the sand, the soles of his shoes crunched. He spoke, but the words meant nothing. Yet they made Samuel pause. He dropped his gaze and moved the knife to his other hand. He licked his lips, tasted sweat. He thought how now would be a good time to do it, to lunge forward and push the knife into the man's belly. But he found that he could not. He was again that man on the pavement, stepping aside for the soldier, that man in the square, loosening his grip so that he did not kill. This was Samuel. A man of weakness. He dropped the knife, gave a coward's cry, turned, and loped toward the cottage. He did not look back to see whether the man had picked up the knife, whether he was chasing him.

He crossed the threshold already falling, his failure pulsing loudly in his ears. He had fled, had run away, given over to a murderer, given up everything he had. He would die. He would die.

But then, as he fell, he saw the front door key. It lay on the carpet in the hallway. It had not been taken. It had been there all along.

Samuel waited several minutes before pulling himself up using the wall. The fall hadn't been hard, but he was winded by it, and his knee had twisted awkwardly under him. He leaned against the jackets hanging on hooks and took a few deep breaths. No one had tripped him this time. He knew that. He had fallen on his own. That other time—at the tower—could he say he had been tripped then? Could he say it hadn't been his own uncertain legs that had done it to him? He was old; his legs were not steady any longer. The man had nothing to do with that. Samuel had allowed paranoia to govern him, allowed himself to believe the man was a criminal without having any proof. But what had the man done that was so bad? Nothing. There was nothing that Samuel could conclusively say the man was guilty of. Not the dead woman nor the threats nor any of the rest.

He tapped his fingers against the wall. He didn't feel well—no, he wasn't well at all. A strange restlessness, light and sharp, coursed through him, and yet despite the motion, it seemed to go nowhere. It was simply shooting, shooting, then dying. He was tired. Bone tired. Nothing, not even that light sharpness, could survive the leaden weariness of age weighing down each part of him.

Outside, the man had returned to his labor. Samuel could hear the collision of stone and metal. He picked up the key where it lay on the sandy carpet and returned it to the lock. He glanced outside. It looked like there would be rain again soon, but he left the door open. He wanted the man to see that, wanted him to come back to that.

He went into the kitchen and packed away the dishes from the previous evening, taking time over it, his arms alive with that disturbing, peculiar current. He boiled water and made a cup of tea, allowing himself three spoons of sugar. There was no knife, so he tore off a piece of the loaf of bread on the counter. It was stale from being left out uncovered, and was hard on his gums, so he dipped it into the tea to soften it. It ought to have been fried, eaten with eggs and tomatoes, but he didn't have the energy for that.

He wondered if the man had eaten yet. There were no crumbs, no dishes, nothing to suggest that he had. Samuel thought of taking tea and bread out to him, but decided against it. He should be more kind, he knew, but it was difficult releasing his pettiness, the resentments and paranoias he had cultivated over the past days.

Difficult with his aged body, the oppressive tower, the long, long past dragging him downward, his mind a confusion of falsehoods and fear.

When he had finished eating and drinking, he wiped down the counter, caught the crumbs in his hand, and leaned out of the window above the sink to throw them away. He went to the living room with a mind to tidying it, but found that there was nothing to do. All had been neatly squared away by the man.

He sat down on the couch a little nervously, still feeling that shooting restlessness fade and return within him. He felt dizzy. It became difficult, impossible, to think clearly. His body ached. He closed his eyes, stiffened, the sharpness in his side growing, moving rapidly, a knife inside him, a knife, a knife. He gasped, grabbing at his side, at his arm, wondering whether he was dying. Was this death? Perhaps he smelled burning. He wasn't sure. He drew his body inward, pulling his legs up to his stomach. He went out of himself then, and he was gone. There was nothing left of him.

He became aware of the sound of hands and tools at work. There was a smell, too, something thick and damp, at odds with what he heard. It was the cloying scent of manure, so strong in the room that his nostrils felt plugged by it. He was still on the couch, though the dizziness and pain of the morning seemed weeks distant. Someone—the man—had placed a blanket over him while he slept. Even so, his hands and feet were cold, very cold, his head hot.

He opened his eyes. The man was on his knees. He had moved the coffee table aside, laid down newspapers to protect the worn carpet. The VCR player had been removed from the chipboard cabinet, leaving the dark memory of its shape marked out by dust.

The smell of manure came in through the open window, but it was closer, too, on the man himself. There were smudges of it on his jersey, brown patches on his knees. He must have been spreading it in the garden. Samuel was grateful; it was a task he had been dreading.

The man looked up from the VCR and smiled at Samuel. He put his head to the side, resting it on both hands in imitation of sleep. He smiled again. Samuel nodded, returned the smile, shrugged.

The man had dismantled the VCR and was fiddling with its parts. He pointed at them with a small yellow-handled screwdriver and spoke a few words. Then he made a gesture, one that surprised Samuel. It was a clenched fist, a raised thumb, a signal that everything was good and going well. It was the first time that Samuel had seen the man using this sign and it made him feel a little bloom of hope where there had previously been none. Here was something valuable: the beginning of a language. It was one thing they had now, one real thing they could say that wasn't pointing and miming. Samuel rubbed his nose, then returned the gesture, a little awkwardly. His fingers couldn't bend fully. The man repeated the sign, laughing.

Samuel pushed himself off the couch, holding on to the arm for a moment as he steadied. It had grown dark inside the cottage; storm clouds had gathered. There came a low rumble of thunder, far off. Samuel switched on the light in the living room so that the man could see better. Then he went into the kitchen and switched on the light there too. He saw with surprise that the knife was lying on the counter, as though it had never left the room, had never threatened anyone.

He put water to boil and took out cups and tea bags. Then he picked up the knife uncertainly; it seemed

lighter now, a useless thing. He used it to trim the edges
of the loaf of bread where he had torn it earlier. He cut
two slices, spread margarine on them with the back of a
spoon he had left in the sink before. He placed the slices
in the frying pan, turning them until each side was
golden brown. He made tea, then carried the warm slices
in one hand, the mugs in the other. He placed the man's
mug and bread on the coffee table on top of a magazine.

The man was busy reconnecting the VCR player to
the television. The screen blinked on, showing nothing
but flashes of white, black, and gray dots. The speakers
hissed with static. The man shook his head at the sound
and rushed to press a button on the set until the noise
lessened and finally there was none at all, just the memory of it still loud between them. He rose from kneeling
and crossed to the bookshelf where Samuel kept the videos. He picked up one, looked at the cover, put it back.
He chose another, and this time he seemed satisfied with
it. There was an electronic gulp as the machine swallowed the tape, and then clicks and notches as the screen
went from pins of dark and light to a second of distorted
images, then, at last, to color. It was an underworld
seascape—fish and shells and rocks. The man fiddled
with the buttons again until there was sound. They
could hear the narration, a woman's voice, speaking
drearily. The man turned around and made the gesture
to ask whether the sound was loud enough. Samuel nodded, returning the thumbs-up.

The two men leaned back on the couch, side by side,

eating and drinking while they watched the documentary. It was something that Samuel had begun watching several months before, when the machine had still been working, but he had stopped shortly after beginning, not being in the mood for it then. It could be a strain to find interest in something on his own. Much easier to go to bed, close his eyes, wait for sleep. But now, with the man beside him making sounds of approval and interest, he found that he was enjoying it, these images of the world beneath the waves.

Samuel had learned over the years what an ungrateful place the island was. How difficult to discipline and nurture. The vegetation was unkind, hard in places, soft as ash in others. It spread where it would, taking over as it wished—yet there were stretches of bleakness where the land was bald and unyielding, a thing of sand and rock. The coastline, too, followed this pattern, its boulders a tumble of seaweed and lichen, or else bare of anything but bird shit and clinging shells. Around them kelp stalks rotted, those brown bodies thrashing in the tide beneath the morning's laggard mist.

When Samuel first came to the island, it was these churning waters that he had feared more than the rest—more than isolation and the strange land. He had said nothing though, had pretended awe at the waves, the vast surrounding sea. The wall, that ever-collapsing wall, had been, perhaps, his attempt at keeping it out, of protecting the land and himself from its onslaught. During the week that his predecessor had introduced him to the island, teaching him the workings of the lighthouse, showing the different shores and beaches, the places to avoid, points of danger, Samuel had felt nothing more threatening than the sea and its relentless approach. He did not like the things it littered on the shore. The plants were easy enough to manage, the smotherweed that choked everything, easy too. It was the sea he wanted tamed.

On a night toward the end of that week, he had been told to dress warmly and to come. He had borrowed an old striped scarf that had once had the badge of a soccer club on it, a team that neither man supported. He was sweating as he followed Joseph down toward the northern shore where the beach was long and narrow, difficult to access from cliff sides made smooth by wind and rain. The old man held a paraffin lantern high for them to see by. The light it cast was dim, turning what it touched into gloom. Samuel struggled to follow, tripping often, and he at one point fell with such a cry that it seemed it must have been heard on the mainland and beyond. Joseph did not falter once, his walk was steady, aided by the stick he carried. He had made it himself, carving a goat's head for the knob, though the horns and snout were rubbed smooth of details by that time. Samuel had the feeling that the old man normally traveled these paths unlit, that the lamp was for Samuel's benefit alone.

Joseph led him over rocks and through crevices until they were standing on the pebbled shore. He snuffed the lamp, leaving Samuel staring blindly into the night. Something was moving out there. Something moving across the beach. He could hear it. A sound that made his back grow cold, made the hair on his arms rise. It was the sound of bones.

"Normally I will catch one," the old man whispered. "Just one, mind, because to catch any more would be a waste. A man can feed on it for days. I cook it up and put it in the cool box and eat as much as I can manage before it spoils. You don't want to eat it once it has begun to turn. You'll be on the toilet for a week."

Samuel blinked. Before him the movements continued, the strange clacking of bone against bone. He thought of skeletons, of all the dead and drowned of the world washing up on the shore. "What are they?" he asked.

"What are they? Haven't you ever seen a crab before? They come here every year at this time, for mating."

Samuel peered into the night. If they were crabs, they were the largest he had ever seen; not in the rivers of the valley nor the market of the city had he ever seen creatures of this size. They moved in a ghastly fashion, their pale forearms waving, waving as they called on the females to mate. Some of the males had begun to duel, clenching hold of one another, dancing from side to side. Mounds grew where several climbed onto a female, forming a slow-moving many-legged and terrifying monster. Already some of the females had begun to molt, crawling out of their shells, their softness gray in the night. Around them was the *clack-clack-clack* of fighting, the sound of limbs breaking, shells splintering.

"No!" he said when the old man moved away from his side, went toward the specters. Joseph had brought a small hatchet slung in his belt, and he used it now, bringing it down on a fat body. The crunch of shell breaking was loud across the beach. Even without light, Samuel could see the fractures, the limbs flailing as the old man began chopping off the legs. When he was done, he nodded at Samuel, "Right, now it's your turn."

"What do you mean?"

"There are two of us. We can have two crabs. Get that big one over there."

Samuel didn't move, though the old man stood holding the hatchet out to him. "Come on, stop wasting time. If you want to live on the island then this is how it is. This is the way we live here. Come on, take it."

He took the hatchet. It was wet, a little slimy. He moved it to his other hand, brought it down in a trial swing. He tried again as he walked toward a molting female. When he hit her, there was almost no sound at all, hardly any resistance. The blade went through her, struck the sand far below. He stumbled, righted himself. The soft parts of her had fallen, but the shell continued to stand.

Afterward Samuel followed the old man back up to the cottage. He carried the lantern now and, like a bundle of wet firewood just collected, the limbs of the two crabs in his arms.

In the kitchen, he watched as the old man began the dissection of the creatures. He cracked the broken shell with his hands and began to pull out meat, pure and white, by the fistful, tossing it into a pot of boiling water for a few minutes before taking it out and replacing it with more. It went on for hours, this process, the table piling up with empty shells, and the smell of the sea hot all around.

As he watched, Samuel found himself deep in the place from which the creatures had emerged, far down in the sunless reaches of the ocean floor, that submerged alien world from which they had made their way to the island for generations. Pushing past the rocks and kelp, the various flotsam and jetsam, moving their ponderous bodies steadily forward, a one-minded approach always to the same point, never altering over the centuries. Some of the crabs were very likely decades old. They were frightening, nightmarish in their size and power. But they were magnificent, too, godlike with their mastery of time and sea and land.

Despite his awe, when invited, Samuel took a handful of the cooked meat, sucked the delicate flesh as easily as inhaling. He had never tasted anything as soft. He reached out for more, licking his fingers even as he chewed, eating until the sun rose and he fell asleep still chewing.

The next year he had done it alone and unafraid. And in this way he had continued for fourteen years, always taking only his allotted one. But still the numbers began to dwindle. Fewer and fewer crabs were returning, until one year they stopped coming altogether.

In the ensuing years, he sometimes took to hovering over rock pools, grabbing crabs no bigger than his palm. He cooked them whole, bit into them to suck out the meat, but found a taste of grainy sand, of rotting seaweed, of rock depths heated by hard sunlight. He craved the monsters of the early years, waited for them, went out at night and called to them by moonlight.

The two men watched the images on the television screen. The events of earlier had been forgotten. There was no malice, no fear or hatred. Samuel had the blanket draped over his knees, a dun cushion on his lap. He was warm, comfortable, and safe. The morning's pains had gone; his head had stopped spinning. He felt only contentment now. Wrapped in the blanket with the man's body next to his, Samuel's head began to nod, his eyelids to fall. He was awake, he could hear the narration of the documentary and the man's breathing, but he was elsewhere too: he was in his family's one-room flat, his infant son on his lap. He held Lesi, rocked him, watched his small face blink and yawn. Here was his son; here was his child. The little boy whom he had never heard speak a word, whom he had never seen walk or crawl. Who had been a newborn for all these long years, never growing, never doing anything but blink and yawn, blink and yawn.

Samuel opened his eyes, saw Lesi sitting beside him

on the couch. A Lesi who had grown into manhood, who had come to help his father in his old age. Samuel put out his hand and placed it over his son's. His throat was thick with tears. There were things he wanted to say. Things he needed to say to his child. He squeezed Lesi's hand. "Thank you for being here. I'm glad you came. I'm glad that I'm not alone anymore."

He wiped a sleeve across his cheeks, fingered tears from his eyes. "I'm glad you came," he said again. Beside him his son smiled, returned the pressure of his hand. Then Lesi moved a little, adjusted his position so that he could put his arm around his father's shoulders. Samuel nodded, began to feel himself drawn back toward the slumber of contentment and warmth. He looked up at Lesi with heavy eyes, began to say something—but his son's face was blurring, and Samuel blinked, watched the features settle themselves into those of the man. Even so, he spoke, said what he had been about to say: "I've been lonely without you."

The man did not reply. He looked away abruptly, removed his arm, sat upright. From outside came the suddenness of squawking, of the chickens forging an assault. And Samuel was awake now, knew what was happening, understood it all. Both men jumped up from the couch at the noise, moved through the room. The man was faster. He was already out of the door and across the yard before Samuel had reached the front door.

A light rain was falling, and Samuel squinted through it as he hobbled after the man. He knew what was happening and he cursed under his breath. The other chickens were attacking the little red hen. He could see the screeching mass of feathers and claws. The man should have known better. She ought not to have been let out. She ought to have been protected. The man had done this.

By now the man was at the attack. He reached inside the tumble of birds to extract the little old hen. There was blood on her, her chest was in tatters. One of her wings would not fold. Around the man, the chickens continued to squawk, making little half-darts at his legs. He kicked out at them, made sounds to chase them away.

"Leave them, leave them!" Samuel called. "Bring her inside! We need to look at her."

But the man did not hear. He remained where he was, holding the little old hen under one arm, and then, fast as blinking, grabbed her neck, twisted it, killed her. Afterward, he raised her body by the feet, leaving her head hanging as he gestured, pointing at his mouth, showing that he would eat her.

Samuel forgot the comfort of company and help. He forgot his yearning for Lesi, for a son with whom to share his island. None of that mattered now. All things within him that had been cowardly turned toward rage. That old call to violence, the call he had never fully believed in, never fully embraced, was growing strong within him.

He reached out to the pile for one of the stones that the man had broken earlier that day, and with the strength of someone he had never before been, he brought the rock down on the side of the man's head. The man was taken by surprise, his mouth became a gaping question as he fell. He dropped the little hen and lay beside her for a moment before trying to push himself back up. The next blow came, and he was lying flat, bringing an arm up to protect himself. But he could not stop it, nor the next, nor any of the strikes that beat into him, each more crushing than the one before, until his face was liquid and scraps. On his left hand a finger twitched, twitched again, then stopped.

Samuel tossed aside the rock, wiped his hands on his jersey. The rain had gone, and the sky was turning toward blue for the first time in days. He moved away from where the body lay, continuing to wipe his hands as he slowly walked back to the cottage. The body could stay there for now. He would put it out to sea tomorrow, leaving it to drift and return to where it had come from.

There was the cry of seabirds, and the roar of waves striking the pebbled shore. It would continue, this relentless ebb and flow, the sea bringing what it chose. Let it come. He crossed the threshold, closing the door of the cottage behind him.

Acknowledgments

I would like to thank Juliano Paccez, Esmarie Jennings, André Krüger, Tochukwu Okafor, and Robert Peett. Most important, I'd like to thank the Miles Morland Foundation for the grant that made writing this book possible and for giving not only financial support but also dignity and respect to writers from Africa.

I would also like to note that an earlier version of the first pages of this novel was published as "Keeping" in Short Story Day Africa's 2017 anthology *Migrations*.

ABOUT THE AUTHOR

KAREN JENNINGS is a South African writer based in Cape Town. She works with the History Department at the University of Stellenbosch, and particularly on the "Biography of an Uncharted People" project. *An Island* is her American debut.

ABOUT THE TYPE

This book was set in Bembo, a typeface based on an old-style Roman face that was used for Cardinal Pietro Bembo's tract *De Aetna* in 1495. Bembo was cut by Francesco Griffo (1450–1518) in the early sixteenth century for Italian Renaissance printer and publisher Aldus Manutius (1449–1515). The Lanston Monotype Company of Philadelphia brought the well-proportioned letterforms of Bembo to the United States in the 1930s.